THE
CASE
OF THE
MURDERED
MACKENZIE

THE CASE OF THE MURDERED MACKENZIE

A MASAO MASUTO MYSTERY

E. V. CUNNINGHAM

DELACORTE PRESS/NEW YORK

Published by
Delacorte Press
1 Dag Hammarskjold Plaza
New York, N.Y. 10017

For Barbara, welcome

1

Detective Sergeant Masao Masuto, his wife, Kati, his twelve-year-old
son, Uraga, and his ten-year-old daughter, Ana, all departed for Japan
on the very same day that Eve Mackenzie—as the subsequent indictment said—murdered her husband. The two events had no connection
other than the fact that Masuto, had he been in Beverly Hills, would
have investigated the murder. As it happened, Masuto was in a Pan Am
plane, high over the Pacific, leaving the investigation to his partner, Sy
Beckman, and to Beckman's boss, Captain Wainwright.

The trip to Japan was something that Masuto and his wife, Kati, had
discussed through the years, not as any sort of reality, but as a pleasant
fantasy. Every dollar they could put aside went into a fund for the
children's college education, and the stories they'd heard of astronomi-
cal hotel and restaurant prices, on top of very expensive airplane fares
kept the Japanese excursion in the area of fantasy. Both Masuto and
Kati were Nisei, which meant they were American-born of Japanese-
born parents. Kati was less eager than her husband to visit the land of
her ancestors. She was a nest-builder, and her own small universe—her
cottage in Culver City, her two children, and her husband—satisfied her
completely.

Masuto, on the other hand, was a Zen Buddhist, and he had often
dreamed of meditating in one of the Zen temples in Kyoto—or perhaps
listening to the wisdom of some famous Roshi, promising himself that
before that unlikely moment arrived, he would do something to correct
his very poor Japanese. However, it arrived very suddenly. His great-
uncle Ishu, who lived in San Jose and who was very old, and who had
little faith in the inheritance laws, sent Masuto a gift of round-trip plane

tickets to Tokyo for his entire family. For a whole evening, Masuto and
his wife debated the pros and cons of the trip, the money that would
have to be spent even if they went only to Tokyo and Kyoto—but what
of other cities where there would be relatives who had to be visited as a
minimal act of courtesy? In the end, agreeing that the opportunity
might never come again, they decided to take the plunge. Masuto had a
month of vacation time coming to him, and he managed to talk Captain
Wainwright, his chief on the Beverly Hills police force, out of another
month, and since it was already late in June, the children would miss
only a few days of school.

The family tour, like all family tours, was both wonderful and de-
pressing. Masuto emerged with new respect for Kati, whose Japanese
was so much better than his, and Kati willingly stayed with the children
while Masuto was guest of honor at a police banquet where, alas, no
wives were present.

The prices were depressingly higher than anything either of them had
anticipated—and for Masuto, his dreams of the pure beauty of Kyoto
was brought down to earth by the sight of a bustling city of over a
million people. As poor as Masuto's spoken Japanese—and perhaps
even worse—was his ability to read the printed Japanese characters;
and since after a few weeks away from California he began to feel
isolated and totally divorced from both past and present, it was indeed
fortunate that Tokyo had several English-language newspapers. It was
there, in the *Japan Times* that he first heard of the Mackenzie affair.

Eve Mackenzie was one of five women who had appeared in a picture
called *The Old Gang,* which was released in 1961. The picture was a
great hit, and all five of the women, who played in a film about a high
school reunion five years later, went on to a sort of stardom. Eve Mackenzie had married Robert Mackenzie just before the film was made. In
the film she played under the name of Eve Hardin. She played in five
more films, became pregnant, lost the child in the seventh month, appeared in a few more films after that, and then eclipsed. That was not
unusual; indeed, that was in the nature of the new Hollywood. Stars
were created and died in less than a lifetime.

Robert Mackenzie, the victim of Eve's passion or anger or frustra-
tion, was Scottish-born, an engineer, brilliant, and when alive employed
at the Fenwick Works, which nestles in the hills to the east of Malibu
and which, as they say, has more millions in war contracts than one can
shake a stick at. The marriage had not been a happy one, and Eve's
friends told reporters that she had been driven to the act. Kati, reading
the account of the crime to Masuto as he sprawled on a couch in their

Tokyo hotel, responded indignantly to the suggestion that anyone might be driven to murder.

"How inhuman! To solve anything with a murder!"

"Yet it is done every day, my dear Kati."

"You justify it? How can you?"

"Of course I don't," Masuto said. "You know me better than that, Kati. Yet our civilization, here as well as at home in the States, has laid the basis for the act and the justification."

"No! How?"

"War. What else is war?"

"You know I can't argue with you about such things. You know that, and you make me feel so foolish."

"My dear Kati, I don't mean to make you feel foolish. You're not. You're a very wise woman." And then he went to her and held her in his arms, which proved his love if not his sincerity.

But he knew that the crux of it was the fact that a murder of major consequence had taken place in Beverly Hills, where murder is certainly not an everyday occurrence, and he had been thousands of miles away. It was the first murder in Beverly Hills in eleven years that he had not investigated.

In Morioka, where he had gone to speak with a Roshi who was an old friend of the Roshi at the Zendo in Los Angeles, he was unable to find an English-language newspaper.

His irritation was such that it caused Bukko, the venerable Zen Roshi he had come to Morioka to meet, to ask Masuto whether there was some serious family difficulty or loss that disturbed him. This question served at least to bring Masuto to his senses.

"I was so mortified before the Roshi," Masuto explained to Kati later, "that I lied to him, and for that I cannot forgive myself."

"But from what you have told me about Zen masters," Kati said gently, "he would know that you were lying."

"Of course he knew."

"Then did you explain to him?"

"What was I to explain to him?" Masuto said unhappily. "It is bad enough to enter a temple and reveal that I am a policeman. Should I add to it the fact that I have become so irritable and unpleasant over a murder committed in Beverly Hills while I am here in Japan?"

"But we are here in Japan," Kati said, "and it is filled with such delightful things. Can we enjoy them—please, Masao?"

"Of course. And I promise you, there will be no further mention of this Mackenzie business."

He kept his word, and he even rejected the notion of a long distance call to his partner, Sy Beckman. This for two reasons: firstly because of its cost, and secondly because he felt it would be both unprofessional and unfriendly to insert himself into the first homicide that Beckman had undertaken alone.

But it was Beckman who brought up the matter of the Mackenzie case after Masuto had reported in on his first day back. Masuto shook hands with his colleagues, responded to the necessary jokes about geisha girls and massage, blew the dust off his desktop, and asked himself whether or not he was pleased to be back in sunny, smog-laced Beverly Hills. He could not help but contrast this quiet, orderly community with the turbulent, explosive and marvelously vital life in Tokyo; yet for all of its gilt-edged lethargy, Beverly Hills had a particular fascination for a policeman. For one thing, it was the largest per capita concentration of wealth in the entire world, and for another, with a population of thirty thousand or so, it contained thirty-five banks, twenty savings and loans, and more jewelry stores than any comparable area anywhere on earth. The gross deposits in Beverly Hills banks amounted to over seven billion dollars, which made the work of a Beverly Hills policeman absolutely unique.

Masuto was always aware of these facts. Rich people are a race, a subculture. Different. "Was he rich?" he asked Beckman, referring to the murdered man, Robert Mackenzie. It was the initial identification.

"What's rich? Compared to us? House on Lexington Road, house at Malibu—that adds up to a couple of million. A million more or so in securities. She's well fixed. Pity she can't use it."

"Pity?"

"Damn it, Masao, I like the woman. And just between us, I don't think she did it." Beckman, a huge, overweight, overmuscled hulk of a man, shook his head with irritation.

"You brought in the evidence," Masuto said gently.

"Hell, it was there. What could I do? So help me God, I wish you had been there, Masao."

"It's your case, Sy. I don't want to interfere."

"Bullshit. Anyway, you can't interfere. Wainwright's closed the book on it. She goes to trial tomorrow, and there's at least a chance they'll convict."

"The case is that good? You know, I've been dependent on the bits and pieces in the Tokyo English-language papers."

"It's good, yes. Not great but good."

"Unseemly haste, as they say. Why so quick to go to trial?"

"Very unseemly. You ask me, she has a pair of lousy lawyers—her husband's lawyers. Can you beat that? Just imagine—her husband's lawyers."

"They may believe she's innocent."

"Not the way I hear it told," Beckman said. "The gossip goes that they don't give a damn and they'd just as soon see her put away for life. Evidently, they've snowed her in some way. Why on God's earth does she use these lawyers? I just don't understand it."

"Why do you think she's innocent?" Masuto asked. "That's more to the point. If you have anything, Sy, put it together and we'll try to make something out of it. Wainwright won't stand in our way."

"I got nothing—nothing. That's why she's on trial, Masao. Please—come into this."

"I'll talk to Wainwright. But with nothing new in the way of evidence, he won't welcome me."

"The woman's on trial," Captain Wainwright told Masuto. "You know, Masao, I damn near cabled you in Japan when this thing broke to tell you to cut off the vacation and come back here. You know the kind of flak we take when there's a murder in Beverly Hills, and this one had to be a hotshot engineer working on some of the fanciest gadgets in the defense field. And done by a movie star. Well, just as well I resisted the temptation. Sy had a full-fledged investigation like this coming to him, and he put together enough for the indictment. It's out of our hands now. We've closed the file."

"We could open it."

"What in hell are you after, Masao?" Wainwright asked angrily. "Because someone else did the investigation? Jealousy?"

"That's not fair, and you know me better than that. Sy thinks she's innocent. He asked me to talk to you."

"You know Beckman when it comes to a beautiful woman. They can do no wrong. And this one's beautiful."

"I also know that Sy's a good cop. He has good insights."

Wainwright sighed and spread his arms. "Who knows? Maybe he's right, maybe he isn't. I got a police department, Masao, and I got to go by the book, and this is no longer a police matter. We made the arrest and we put together the evidence and we turned it over to the district attorney. Now it's out of our hands. Let the court decide, which is why we got a thing called trial by jury. I don't want to hear any more about it. I'm glad you're back, Masao, but maybe getting into one of these damned arguments with you isn't the best way to start off."

"No argument, Captain. It's your position, and it's plain enough."

Back in his office, where Beckman was waiting, Masuto shook his head. "No go. He says it's out of our hands."

Beckman shrugged. "He's right."

"I think he's mellowing," Masuto said. "Time was when he would have bitten my head off for even suggesting that a case in court should be reopened for investigation. Anyway, after that case where a film star took a few too many and then fell off a yacht and drowned, and the investigation was squeezed right out of existence—"

"Not to mention the Belushi case—"

"They were off our turf, but someone has to pay the piper, and I'm afraid it's Eve Mackenzie. She's the symbol of a blind justice that chooses no favorites, rich or poor or whatever, except when she's already been hurt too much for the rich and famous."

"And don't think the jury won't be licking their lips over that."

"You think she'll be convicted?"

"And not with my smarts, Masao. She lined it all up against herself."

"Deliberately?"

"No . . ." He hesitated. "No, I don't think so. It just came together that way. You know, someone who's not in our business will give you a lot of mathematical crap about the improbability of coincidence. But I've seen too many coincidences to look at it that way."

"And this case is loaded with them?"

"You can say that again."

"There is one thing," Masuto said thoughtfully. "The laws of probability are based on reality. Sometimes they appear to break down, but sometimes they're tampered with."

Beverly Hills, a self-governing and independent city possessed of its own fire department, its own police department, its own school system, and its own table of social and civic services, is nevertheless totally surrounded by the City of Los Angeles. A number of communities in Los Angeles are in a similar situation—one which possibly exists nowhere else in the nation—and in the case of Beverly Hills, the judicial system reaches only as far as a municipal court. Criminal cases are tried in the nearest superior court, in this instance in Santa Monica, which nestles along the Pacific shore about ten miles from Beverly Hills.

It was there, in Santa Monica, that Detective Sy Beckman had to appear as witness for the prosecution. As his superior in the tiny Beverly Hills homicide bureau, Detective Sergeant Masao Masuto went with him—tentatively, since he expected Wainwright to demand what the hell Masuto was needed for out there in Santa Monica.

But Wainwright said nothing. It was a very quiet moment in the criminal history of Beverly Hills—no assaults, only two robberies, no purse-snatchings.

"It's routine," Beckman said. "You'd be here anyway if we'd both done the investigation."

"No. He's gone soft."

"Not Wainwright."

"Do you realize he's given me the day off?"

"Come on," Beckman said. "You're going to sit in that courtroom. What kind of a day off is that?"

"The kind I'm looking forward to," Masuto said.

"You been reading. You think she's innocent?"

"I wish I could understand why you think so."

"Maybe I dream about leaving my wife and staking out a pup tent on Malibu Beach with Eve Mackenzie. God knows why!"

Masuto knew Beckman's wife. He could understand Beckman's feelings, and recalling Eve Mackenzie's beauty on the screen, he found that her films did not exaggerate the attraction of the living woman. How could one look at the comely and charming woman sitting at the defense table and think of her as a murderer? Beckman was outside in the witness room, which gave Masuto a chance to watch Eve Mackenzie undisturbed—the pale but good skin in this land of forced tan and sunburn, calm, wide gray eyes, ash-blond hair that might just have been natural, and no pretensions to less than her forty-one years. What would describe her? And then he caught an answer. Dignity. She was possessed of a calm and unusual dignity. Possibly she was playing a role, since she was a gifted actress; if so, she was playing it very well.

Her lawyers arrived in court, one of them a heavyset, thick-featured man in his fifties—that would be either Cassell or Norman—and the other, one of those bright young men who finds a place in the best legal firms, cut from proper cardboard, with a proper head and nose and mouth, interchangeable with ten thousand others. As people filed into the courtroom, Masuto heard the name Cassell addressed to the heavyset man. But why Cassell? Why did the dead man's attorneys choose to defend the accused murderer of their one-time client? Beckman's explanation was that Cassell and Norman had been family attorneys; but that was hardly good enough to satisfy Masuto.

The judge entered, Judge Harry Simpkins, firm but human as Masuto saw him. The jury was in place, eight women, four men—too many women, too many of them old and bitter. Everyone rose. The judge seated himself and the court sat down. The judge had white hair. Passion lay somewhere in his past.

Today, Beckman was the first witness. "Call Seymour Beckman!" the clerk announced.

It always gave Masuto a start to have Beckman identified as Seymour. The big, slope-shouldered detective went poorly with his name. He was big but not clumsy; he moved like an athlete as he came down the aisle and took his place in the witness box. The clerk took his oath, and then Mark Geffner, the district attorney, began the questioning. Masuto had worked with Geffner in the past. Geffner was not brilliant, but decent, straightforward, and honest.

"State your name and position, please," he said to Beckman.

"Seymour Beckman, detective, Beverly Hills police force."

"How long have you been with the Beverly Hills Police Department?"

"Sixteen years."

"And how long with homicide?"

"When Detective Sergeant Masuto was assigned full-time to Homicide, I was given the assignment of working with him. When he needed me. That was nine years ago."

"And in the case of the Mackenzie murder, I take it that Detective Masuto was out of the country."

Cassell was on his feet with a bellow of objection.

"On what grounds?" the judge asked mildly.

"The state has not yet proven that Robert Mackenzie was murdered. We hold that his death was accidental."

"Quite so." The judge nodded and said to Geffner, "Remember that, please, Mr. Geffner." He then told the stenographer to strike it from the record. Masuto's impression was that the judge would be meticulously fair. Since the courtroom was loaded with reporters and artists, everyone—judge, attorneys, defendant, and jury—must have been conscious of playing roles in a national drama.

"Nevertheless," Geffner said, "you were in charge of the investigation."

"Yes, sir."

"Would you tell us, Detective Beckman, what happened on the day of June twenty-second."

Beckman took out his notebook but did not consult it immediately. "I signed in at the police station at a few minutes before eight A.M. At about eight-thirty, Captain Wainwright—"

"Would you identify Captain Wainwright?"

"Chief of Detectives—also the head of the force. Well, he told me that there was a situation at the Mackenzie home on Lexington Road that might or might not be a homicide. It had been reported as an accident, but the ambulance from All Saints Hospital—I mean the men on the ambulance—they certified Mr. Mackenzie as dead and were unwilling to remove the body until our medical examiner, Dr. Sam Baxter, had seen it."

"Yes, just what were these suspicious circumstances, Detective Beckman."

"If you would let me tell it my way," Beckman said, consulting his notebook now.

"Yes, of course."

"I left for the Mackenzie house immediately. It's on Lexington, just past Benedict Canyon Drive. I knew the house. It's part of my work to know most of the houses that important people live in. When I got there, Officer Keller was sitting in his car in the driveway, waiting for me. It's general practice to have a car standing by in a situation like this, even if there's no hard evidence yet of a crime. The ambulance had left, but I saw Dr. Baxter's car in the driveway."

"Is Dr. Baxter the same man who did the subsequent autopsy?"

"Yes. We don't have a regular pathology department in Beverly Hills. We use All Saints' pathology room and morgue. When we need him, Dr. Baxter acts as our medical examiner."

"Yes. Go on, please."

"I spoke to Officer Keller, and he informed me that only the housekeeper and Dr. Baxter were in the house."

"Would you identify the housekeeper, please."

"Feona Scott, widow, thirty-nine years old, been with the Mackenzies four years."

"You went into the house then?"

"Yes, sir," Beckman said. "I went into the house. That is, Mrs. Scott opened the door for me and told me that Mr. Mackenzie's body was upstairs in the main bedroom. She directed me to the bathroom off the master bedroom and separated from it by a dressing room. As I entered the master bedroom, Dr. Baxter yelled at me to tell Mrs. Scott to phone All Saints and get the ambulance back here. I asked him whether that meant that Mackenzie was alive. I'm afraid it meant that Mackenzie was dead and he wanted the ambulance to take the body to the pathology room."

Masuto smiled, thinking of what Baxter had probably said, something to the effect of, Alive as you are from the neck up. Baxter was hardly a pleasant person, and he regarded every homicide as a personal affront to his time and dignity.

"I then asked Dr. Baxter what was the cause of death, and he said that until he did an autopsy he was guessing. Possibly Mr. Mackenzie had been electrocuted while taking a bath. However, he indicated an ugly bruise at the deceased's temple. Dr. Baxter suggested that a small radio in the bathroom might have been the cause of electrocution if he had been electrocuted—that it might have either been thrust into the tub or fallen into the tub. He also said that the blow to the head might have killed Mackenzie."

Cassell rose to object to this as provocative guesswork and hearsay, and the judge asked Beckman whether he could substantiate his statements. Before he could answer, Geffner announced that he intended to call Dr. Baxter and both ambulance attendants as witnesses. "Detective Beckman," Geffner said, "just tell us what happened without any inferences or suggestions."

"I was only telling you what Dr. Baxter said."

"I understand. Please go on."

"Well, I know a little something about electricity, and when you've been a cop as long as I have, you seen practically everything, and we had incidents where an electric appliance had fallen into a tub or a pool. The radio in the bathroom was wet, and when I shook it I could hear water sloshing around inside. At the same time, the light in the bathroom was still working. It's possible for someone with a bad heart to be killed by an appliance dropped into a tub, but one expects the appliance to blow the fuse or snap the circuit breaker. So the first thing I thought about was where was the fuse box. I asked Mrs. Scott, and she led me to it. I opened it. It was the old-fashioned kind of fuse box, not circuit breakers, and there were notations for each fuse. But the fuse next to the bathroom label had been removed, and in its place a copper penny had been inserted."

At this point Geffner said, "Excuse me, Detective Beckman. It is possible that some members of the jury are unaware of what this signifies. Would you explain to them."

"A fuse is a safety device," Beckman told the jury. "So is a circuit breaker, but the circuit breaker is an improvement because it's hard to tamper with. The purpose of a fuse is to limit the amount of electricity that can be drawn over a single circuit. When the electrical demand exceeds the bearing capacity of the fuse, the fuse blows out and breaks the circuit. Without fuses we'd have an endless stream of fires—in fact, I guess you couldn't have electric power without fuses or circuit breakers. But if you want a real shot of electric power, you can take out the fuse and replace it with a conductor—in this case, a copper penny. But there's one catch to that, and a very dangerous one. If the radio had dropped into the tub and was left there, at some point the wiring would have burst into flame—unless someone had unplugged the radio cord within a minute or so after it was put into the tub."

Cassell objected and Geffner fought back, and Judge Simpkins called both of them up to the bench and told Cassell that a scientific fact was not an unfounded premise. "On the other hand," he said to Geffner, "I presume you will put an electrical engineer on the stand?"

"That has been arranged for, Your Honor."

"Then let the engineer go into the scientific background and hold Beckman to what he saw and did."

Geffner then asked Beckman what his next step was.

"I telephoned Captain Wainwright, and I told him that the Mackenzie thing had every appearance of being a homicide. You see, Dr. Baxter wanted the ambulance from All Saints to pick up Mackenzie's body, but that would only wash if we were dealing with a homicide. If it was an accidental or medical death, it would be up to the family where they wanted the body taken or whether they wanted an autopsy."

"But at that moment, Detective Beckman, there was no family present?"

"No, sir. Only Mrs. Scott. Mrs. Mackenzie came home about a half hour later. She said—"

"Never mind what Mrs. Mackenzie said. We'll get to that later. I want to know what happened after you telephoned Captain Wainwright."

"Well, he said to leave the body where it was, in the tub, until we could contact someone in the family. Then Mrs. Scott—"

"The housekeeper."

"Yes, sir. Then Mrs. Scott brought me Mrs. Mackenzie's notebook."

"Did you ask for it?"

"No, sir. At that point I didn't know of its existence."

Geffner handed Beckman a black vinyl-covered looseleaf notebook. "Is this the notebook in question?"

"Yes, sir."

"How can you be sure without opening it?"

"It has my mark—that bit of tape."

"Would you glance through it just to make sure."

Beckman glanced through the notebook, after which Geffner entered it as evidence.

"Officer Beckman, did you ask Mrs. Scott whether she knew the contents of the notebook?"

"Subsequently, I did."

"And what was her answer?"

"She said she did not know what was in the notebook, but since she suspected that Mrs. Mackenzie had killed her husband—"

Cassell was on his feet, objecting angrily. The judge called him and Geffner up to the bench, where Cassell whispered hoarsely, "This is unconscionable. Mrs. Scott is not on the witness stand, and her opinion is not evidence, and when you put her opinion in the mouth of a homicide detective, you do my client an irreparable injury."

"I don't think so," Simpkins said gently. He was a soft-voiced man, white-haired and fatherly. "However, I shall sustain your objection and instruct the jury to ignore Beckman's answer."

"Your Honor," Geffner said, "that notebook is central to the people's case—"

"Softly, Mr. Geffner. No one is attacking the notebook. There are other ways to get at its contents."

The judge instructed the jury to ignore Mrs. Scott's opinion, and Geffner said to Beckman, "We will return to the notebook later, but at this point, Detective Beckman, I would like to stay with the sequence of events so that the jury may have a clear idea of what you saw that morning at the Mackenzie home. You have testified that Captain Wainwright of the Beverly Hills police instructed you to go there to look into what might or might not have been a homicide—"

"Are you summing up so early in the trial, Mr. Geffner?" the judge asked gently.

"No, Your Honor. But this is a complicated sequence of events. I am trying to clarify it."

"I think that proper questioning will simplify it and clarify it."

Geffner nodded and referred to his notes. "About what time was it that Mrs. Scott gave you the notebook?"

"It was exactly nine fifty-one."

"How can you say exactly, Detective Beckman?"

"In a homicide investigation, I note the time if something happens that I consider of importance."

"And you considered the notebook a matter of importance?"

"After Mrs. Scott—"

Geffner anticipated Cassell's objection. "Simply yes or no, Detective Beckman."

"Yes."

Geffner was making a timetable for his own use. "You left the police station about eight-forty, arrived at the Mackenzie home before nine, made your investigation, and received the notebook at nine fifty-one. Is that correct?"

"Yes, sir."

"And what time did Mrs. Mackenzie arrive at the house?"

"Ten thirty-three."

"I presume that once again you noted the time and consulted your watch?"

"Yes, sir."

"And since we're being precise about time, Detective Beckman, in the forty-two minutes that elapsed between Mrs. Scott handing you the notebook and Mrs. Mackenzie arriving home, did you have any opportunity to digest at least part of its contents?"

"I don't know what I digested," Beckman replied. "Mrs. Scott practically insisted that I begin to read the notebook right then and there."

"Did she? How very interesting. Now, let's get back to Mrs. Mackenzie. Did the officer outside make her aware of what had happened?"

"Well, I opened the door for her. She knew something had happened. She asked me who I was. I told her and showed identification. Then I told her there had been an accident and her husband was dead."

"How did she react to this information?"

"She was cold and—maybe you'd call it withdrawn—"

Cassell was already on his feet, objecting.

"On what grounds, Mr. Cassell?" the judge asked patiently.

"This witness is a policeman. He is not competent to analyze a person's reactions on the basis of a facial expression."

"I'm not asking for an analysis," Geffner argued. "The question is how does a person look. We ask and answer that question every day of our lives."

"I tend to agree with that. I'm going to let it stand."

Geffner thanked the judge and then had the stenographer read the question and answer.

"You said cold and withdrawn, Detective Beckman. Could you elaborate on that?"

"Well, ordinarily if you inform a woman that her husband has been badly hurt or killed, which I have had to do at times, she has a violent reaction."

"Explain what you mean by a violent reaction, please."

"Hysteria, screaming, fainting—sometimes just a frozen sort of paralysis."

"And Mrs. Mackenzie's reaction was none of these."

"No, none of them. I told her that her husband was dead. She nodded. Then she asked how it happened. Did someone kill him? I asked her why she should think so, and she replied that with a house full of cops, it was more or less evident. Then she asked me again how it had happened. I told her, and then she nodded and shrugged her shoulders."

Cassell was on his feet again, demanding that this testimony be stricken as prejudicial. "This policeman is, in fact," he shouted, "telling the jury that my client is a soulless person. On what basis? On the basis of the fact that her husband's death drew a particular response from her!"

"That's enough, Mr. Cassell," Judge Simpkins said. "My hearing is excellent. There is absolutely nothing improper about this testimony and I intend to allow it to stand. You will have your turn with Detective Beckman. Until then, I suggest you be patient."

"And then, Detective Beckman?" Geffner asked.

"I told her that the ambulance from All Saints Hospital would be there in a few minutes to pick up the body, and that since there was reason to believe that a crime had been connected with her husband's death, an autopsy was scheduled, but if she wanted to get in touch with her lawyers, she could have the autopsy postponed. She said, no, she had no objection. Then I asked her whether she wanted to see her husband's body. She said, yes, she would."

"And where was the body at that point in the sequence of events?" Geffner asked.

"It was still in the tub. Dr. Baxter said that rigor mortis had already set in and that we might as well leave it where it was until the ambulance arrived. We covered it with a sheet."

"I presume that the water had been let out of the tub?"

"Yes, sir."

"You told Mrs. Mackenzie where her husband's body was?"

"Yes, sir."

"What was her reaction to that?"

"She just shook her head and mumbled something about her husband not using the tub—something about him taking showers. I led the way to the bathroom. Dr. Baxter had already left the house. Joe Garcia, one of our officers, was stationed outside the bathroom door."

"This was a large upstairs bathroom—the master bathroom?"

"Yes, sir, there are five bathrooms in the Mackenzie house, if you count the powder room. This one had to be entered through the master bedroom."

"All right. Continue."

"I mentioned that her husband was naked but covered with a sheet and I asked her if she wanted me to go into the bathroom with her. She said she'd rather go in alone. She left the door open, and from outside I saw her pull the sheet off and stare at the body in the tub. She was a very cool lady. She turned around and left the bathroom, and as she came out, she said—"

Geffner tried to stop Beckman with "You can—" but let it go when he realized that it was too late.

" 'That dead man is not my husband,' " Beckman finished.

The reporters in the courtroom broke for the door in a mad rush, while the judge pounded his gavel for order.

Masuto had listened carefully to every word of testimony, and this last bit, the statement by Mrs. Mackenzie, via Beckman, that the dead man was not her husband, intrigued him completely. What had been, so far as the newspapers had reported it, a straightforward and mundane Hollywood scandal, now showed indications of becoming something else entirely. Masuto was interested and fascinated, but examining the source of his own interest, and given to a good deal of introspection, he wondered whether it was not simply the woman who fascinated him— the woman whose control allowed her to walk into that bathroom without hysteria or apparent fear.

Geffner sighed and said, "I would like you to repeat Mrs. Mackenzie remark, now that it's on the record."

"She said, 'That dead man is not my husband.' "

"You were interrupted before. Please go on."

"I asked her what she meant. I told her that the body had been identified by Mrs. Scott, who told us it was her husband. Then she kind of snorted and shrugged."

"Snorted?"

"Like this." Beckman gave an imitation of someone snorting. "Then I asked her where she had been."

"Yes? Go on, Detective Beckman."

"She asked me if she was under arrest. For what, I asked her. Then she said—" he consulted his notebook—" 'everything around here points to the fact that you people believe someone has been murdered.' "

"Did she refer to her husband?"

"Not at that time, no. Later—"

"We'll take later in due time. Please stay with the sequence of events."

"Yes, sir. At that moment Mr. Cassell arrived."

"You mean Henry Cassell, Mrs. Mackenzie's attorney."

"Yes, sir. The gentleman sitting there." Beckman pointed to the defense table.

"Do you know who had called him to the house?"

"I did not then. Subsequently, I learned that Mrs. Scott had telephoned his office and left a message for him to come to the Mackenzie house as soon as he arrived."

"Very well. Mr. Cassell arrived. What then?"

"He demanded to know who I was. I identified myself. He then told

Mrs. Mackenzie that she did not have to speak to me or answer any questions, and she said she would like to go to her room, and he said she could, and then she noticed her notebook, which I had left on a small credenza. She grabbed it, very angry. I told Mr. Cassell that it was evidence in a criminal situation, and he persuaded her to let me have it. She was disturbed and she went to her room. I guess she was very disturbed."

Geffner looked at Cassell, waiting for an objection, but he said nothing.

"And then, Detective Beckman?"

"Mr. Cassell asked me if he could see the deceased. I then took him upstairs. Mrs. Mackenzie was at the door of her room, which would be the master bedroom. But she said she would lie down in her room."

"Do you mean the master bedroom? You identified that as her room."

"No. I meant that it was a bedroom I thought she and her husband both used because it was the master bedroom. But I learned that they slept in separate rooms."

"Then it was not to the room with the body that she went?"

"No, sir. She was just standing there next to the policeman who was on duty there. Then she walked down the hall to her own room. Mr. Cassell and I went into the master bedroom and then into the bathroom where the deceased was. I removed the sheet and Mr. Cassell looked at the body."

"How did he look at it? I mean, did he simply glance at the corpse or what?"

"No, sir. He stood there for quite a bit of time before he asked me to cover the deceased again."

"Did you tell him what Mrs. Mackenzie had said?"

"I did. He said the deceased was Robert Mackenzie, no question about it. I asked him why he thought the defendant said what she said, but he could offer no explanation."

At this point the court broke for lunch.

4

"There is a rather good Japanese restaurant on Ocean Avenue," Masuto told Beckman. "It hides itself in one of those old Victorian houses. That's a syndrome we still carry over from World War II. An unwillingness to be noticed. But if we get a table at the window, we can look out over the ocean."

"I'm starved, so if the tempura's good, I'm with you. I'm not made for the job, Masao. I'm a lousy witness."

"Not so. You're a good, straightforward witness. That's the best kind of a witness to have. It's not you—it's this damn strange situation of the Mackenzies."

Masuto was able to park directly in front of the restaurant, and the owner, flattered by Masuto's patronage, gave them the best table at the front windows. This was not difficult, since only two other tables were occupied; nevertheless, they could look through the palms to where the sun glistened on the Pacific. They had two hours before they had to return to the court.

"A very large plate of tempura for my friend," Masuto said. "For myself, I'll have sushi. Rice and tea. No sake so early in the day."

"I wanted to help her," Beckman said, "but every word I spoke tied the rope tighter."

Masuto was watching the gulls, bemused by the birds' incredible eyesight. To see made a seer. The gulls were seers.

"Who else identified the body?" he asked Beckman.

"You know, I try to think the way you think. I'm not putting myself down, Masao, but we've been a lot of years together. They had taken the body over to the pathology room at All Saints, but I persuaded four of the men from Fenwick who had worked with Mackenzie to come to All Saints and look at the body."

"What did they say? Was it Mackenzie?"

"No question about it. I wasn't easily satisfied, Masao. I'm not as thorough as you are, but I tried to be."

"Stop apologizing."

"I compared photographs. The family doctor came to All Saints. He's a Dr. Sheperdson from Westwood. He identified the body."

Their food came.

"Let's eat," Masuto said. "Plenty of time to talk about it. Out there" —he gestured through the window at the ocean—"all is very peaceful. A very beautiful place. I have heard that it is like the south of France. I've never been to France, never anywhere in Europe, and yet all that distance to Japan."

"I never had a chance to ask you about the trip," Beckman said, his mouth full of fried shrimp.

"A very interesting trip. Very much so. And still she insisted that it was not her husband?"

"The Mackenzie woman?"

Masuto nodded.

"At first. Then she clammed up on that. Then she came back to it after we arrested her."

"Why?"

"Why?"

"I mean, why did you arrest her? I read her story in the papers. She had a fight with her husband, whom she apparently detested. She stormed out of the house—her claim at midnight—and then drove to Santa Barbara, where she spent the night with her sister. Then back to the house in the morning."

"She claims, to pack her stuff and leave him."

"So it comes down to the notebook, doesn't it? What's in the notebook?"

"The whole story of the murder, very precise, very specific."

"No!"

"Absolutely."

"And you kept it away from the press?"

"That wasn't easy, Masao, but that's the way Geffner wanted it."

"What was in the notebook?"

"She was writing a screenplay," Beckman said somewhat sadly. "And it wasn't just something she put up as an alibi. It was a screenplay, and the whole shtick was in there, the penny in the fuse box, the radio in the bathtub—"

"Come on!" Masuto exclaimed, pushing away his plate of food. "That's it?"

"I know it's circumstantial."

"Circumstantial! It's not even a shadow of a case. Unless there's something you haven't told me."

"Background stuff. She hated her husband. Constant fights. He beat her up once or twice. He threatened to kill her if she ever decided to leave him. Some kind of sex relationship between Mackenzie and this Feona Scott—although to my way of thinking, given a choice between that Scott dame and Eve Mackenzie, I wouldn't have to think twice."

"All this information supplied by the helpful Feona Scott?"

"Yes."

"What was Doc Baxter's guess about the time of the murder?"

"You know Baxter. It's hard enough to get an opinion on time of death in the best of circumstances. In a bathtub—well, was the water hot or cold? Did it remain in the tub? How long? All he would commit to was that Mackenzie died sometime between midnight and five in the morning."

"And when did Eve leave the house?"

"She doesn't know. Never looked at her watch. Maybe around midnight."

"And what does the helpful Scott say?"

"She hates Eve Mackenzie. She's one of those tall, cold types—as emotional as a fish. She brought me the notebook. She says Eve left the house well after one in the morning."

"It's meaningless. It's all senseless. Who the devil ordered the arrest? Was it Wainwright?"

"You know him better than that. It was the D.A."

"Geffner?"

"That's right."

"That's crazy, Sy. I know Geffner. He's too smart for anything like this. And why the devil would he come into Beverly Hills and ask for an arrest?"

"Beats me. I couldn't make head or tail out of that."

"You know," Masuto said with pleasure, "this case grows more interesting by the minute. Let's finish eating and spend a half hour in the sun."

They walked along Ocean Avenue, found a bench that sat on top of the high cliff facing the ocean and dulling the roar of traffic from the Pacific Coast Highway below them.

"So Geffner persuaded Wainwright to issue the arrest order," Masuto said. "Will wonders never cease?"

"I don't follow you," Beckman said uneasily. "I figured the case was open and shut."

"You're in love with Eve Mackenzie. You are a hopeless romantic, Sy."

"Come on."

"So are a hundred thousand others," Masuto said gently. "That got in the way. You were sure that Geffner would hound her to surrender and that an angry jury would convict. No way. Sy, this case is never going to get to a jury. The judge will throw it out."

"Why?"

"Because it's full of holes and without a shred of worthy evidence."

"But look at the way it lines up. She never meant for that notebook to be found. A week before, she tossed it into the garbage to be rid of it."

"Let me guess. Feona Scott found it—just happened to be rooting in the garbage that day."

"You're making me feel like a damn fool, Masao."

"No, sir. You followed a chain of events. You were caught up in them. You were supposed to."

"I was supposed to use my head. The same evidence would point to Scott. But she had no motive—what do you mean, I was supposed to? You think she was framed?"

"I don't know what to think at this moment," Masuto said, "except that this is a damn strange bundle of facts. Start with Geffner. We've seen him operate. He's smart, and he goes in like a tiger. Today, he was diddling. He knows the judge is going to dump it."

"You could be wrong."

"We'll see. Meanwhile, Eve Mackenzie is defended by the dead man's lawyer. Next point: She says the dead man is not her husband. How do you explain that?"

"I figured she was desperate," Beckman said. "Just pulled something from out of the hat."

"It would be a lunatic kind of desperation, and she's no lunatic. The reality is always there, but we refuse to look at it. Or we look at it and refuse to see it. If she insists that the dead man is not her husband and everyone else insists that he is, then we must look at the reality as she does. By the way, from the way the press reacted today, I would suppose that you've kept that business quiet."

"About the corpse not being Mackenzie?"

Masuto nodded.

"She kept it quiet after her first statement."

"Ah, so," Masuto said softly. "We come to the first bit of sanity in an otherwise senseless picture. If she were under the illusion that she would have a real trial, then it would be very smart indeed to keep that bit of information quiet. Then Cassell puts her on the stand and she proves that the dead man is not Mackenzie. Thus, no motive. Thus, she is on trial for killing a man who may not be dead. Thus, down the drain with the case. But neither she nor Cassell could have anticipated a real trial. After all, Cassell is a smart lawyer."

"And how was she going to prove that Mackenzie was not Mackenzie?" Beckman was smiling.

"You couldn't get his fingerprints," Masuto said.

"Exactly. Fenwick builds missile components and the plumbing for atomic bombs. All that top secret crap. I asked for a comparison with the dead man's prints, and they said to send them a set of his prints. I asked for a Xerox of the prints card from their records, and they said they don't do things that way, but to send them a set of prints and they'd make the comparison."

"You did it, and they said it was Mackenzie."

"Masao, I'm a damn fool, and maybe I'd give every cent I got to spend a weekend with Eve Mackenzie, but that's not why when she says it's not her husband I believe her. You said before that we should look at the reality as she does. What do you mean by that?"

"Everyone else who looked at the corpse said it was Mackenzie. But when Eve Mackenzie looked at the body she saw something that was meaningless to the others. She saw a naked man. None of the others had ever seen Mackenzie naked—"

"Scott?"

"Believe me, whatever goes on there, Scott is in on it. Her testimony is tainted. But the others identified a man clothed. Only Eve knew the naked Mackenzie, and she saw something, perhaps a birthmark, that made her certain. Was there a birthmark?"

"I just don't know. I wasn't looking for one. But if it wasn't Mackenzie—"

"It was someone who looked enough like him to be his twin brother. And that's precisely what we have, a corpse that is Mackenzie's twin brother."

"That doesn't make any sense either," Beckman said. "But at this point, maybe none of it does." He looked at his watch. "Time's up. You coming back to court with me?"

"No. I think I'll talk to Doc Baxter."

"The pleasure is all yours," Beckman said.

5

It took Masuto about twenty minutes to drive from Santa Monica to All Saints Hospital. The pathology room was in the basement, where the odor of formaldehyde substituted for air and where two grinning, bearded young men assisted Dr. Baxter. Baxter himself, short, waspish, astringent, always worked up his general state of unpleasantness at the sight of a policeman. He considered it an act of ungenerous fate that chose All Saints as the Beverly Hills replacement for a real morgue and himself as a part-time medical examiner; and now he regarded Masuto sourly.

"I heard you had gone off to the home of your ancestors. What brings you back?"

Masuto resisted the impulse to say that it was an ill wind or Pan Am. Baxter had to be handled gently and with a certain degree of humility if one desired anything in return, and Masuto told him that he was pleased to be back, and being back, was interested in the Mackenzie case.

"Well, bless your heart. Can't stand it that one got away from you."

"I'm curious. Where's the body?"

"The body. Now, what did you imagine, my Oriental friend, that I'd have it sitting here in the icebox against the possibility that you'd return one day and ask to contemplate it?"

"I merely asked."

"Indeed. Well, I have to inform you that Mr. Robert Mackenzie, having gone to his reward, whatever that may be, is reposing quietly about six feet below the surface of that Rolls Royce of all cemeteries, namely Forest Lawn, where the Mackenzies have a family plot. Ah, thus liveth and dieth the rich."

"When you did the autopsy," Masuto said, "did you notice anything unusual—some birthmark or such—on the body where the clothes would have covered it."

Baxter looked at him shrewdly. "You got some smarts, Masuto. I give you credit for that. You're wondering why she took one look and said it wasn't her husband. But suppose nothing was there?"

"Then it was the absence of something, which amounts to the same thing. Suppose it was an operation. What's most likely?"

"Appendectomy."

Masuto sighed and shook his head.

"You could cover the L.A. hospitals," Baxter said. "That's not impossible. Of course, it could have been done twenty years ago. How old was Mackenzie—fifty-three? It might have been done when he was a kid. And I can assure you that the corpse had no surgery—large or small."

Masuto shook his head again. "It's pretty hopeless. But one other thing. There was a blow to the head."

"Skull fracture."

"Would the blow have rendered him unconscious?"

"Absolutely. In fact, odds are that it killed him."

"The blow was on the right side?"

"You're a real smartass detective, aren't you, Masuto. And Mackenzie was sitting with his right side against the wall. So if his wife knocked him out, she had to lean over behind him. I told that to your brainless partner, but he has imagination. He said that if Mackenzie had twisted around to talk to his wife, she could have hit him there. Just turn around a little more, sweetheart, and bend your head so I can knock your brains out. Cops! God help us with that kind of law and order! Tell you something, they subpoenaed me as a witness and I'm going to blow this case right out of the courtroom."

"I'm sure you will," Masuto agreed. "Very grateful. Thank you."

It was good to be out of there, back in the fresh air, away from the stink of open bodies and formaldehyde. Masuto drove to the police station at Rexford Drive in Beverly Hills. After parking at the station, he sat in his car for a few minutes brooding over as essentially wrong a situation as he had ever encountered. Then he stepped into the sunshine that almost always bathed Beverly Hills, and then he went into the police station.

Captain Wainwright had locked his office door, enjoying his after-lunch cigar in premises where smoking was forbidden. Masuto could smell it seeping under the door, whereby he knocked and named himself at the same time. Wainwright opened the door and asked what his business was. "I'm still out to lunch," he said.

"We have to talk."

"You were out in Santa Monica. I told you to take the day and sit in court and hold Beckman's hand. You going to look a gift horse in the mouth?"

"That's right. This horse has three legs."

"I do declare, Masuto, that you can make my life as miserable as a dog's hind side on an anthill, and I damn well do know what you're going to say. Leave it alone. Why the hell couldn't you stay another week in Japan?"

"We got a funny city, Captain, and a lot of rich people, and we're sort of a freak as cities go, and we got Rodeo Drive, where a man can buy a shirt for two hundred dollars and a suit for twelve hundred dollars, and we have the highest-priced hookers in the world, and we got houses that sell for three million dollars, but I never heard anyone accuse us of having dirty cops. They accuse Beverly Hills of everything else, but not a crooked police force."

"You're going too far, Masao. I've put up with damn near everything from you—"

"Just tell me why you arrested and charged Eve Mackenzie, and I'll swallow everything I said."

"I don't have to tell you one damn thing!"

"So sorry, Captain Wainwright." Masuto turned and opened the door.

"Where the hell are you going? And don't give me any of that Charlie Chan routine!"

"I'm going to sit in my office and decide whether I want to work here anymore."

"Close that door and stop being a horse's ass!" There was a slight smile on Masuto's face that disappeared as he turned around. "Now, sit down," Wainwright said to him. "Talk. Get it off your chest."

"All right. I listened to Beckman's testimony. Then I had lunch with him. Then I went over to see Doc Baxter. He's going to testify that there's no way in the world Eve Mackenzie could have killed her husband."

"I know that."

"You know that, and you withheld it from Beckman. Sy Beckman's been my partner for years. He has more courage and decency than any man I ever worked with, and you've made a fool of him, and you've withheld evidence from him and you made him the arresting officer in as rotten and ridiculous a case as I've ever seen."

"That's so."

"Why?"

"I don't have to tell you why, Masao, and don't push me. I'm tired of being pushed. What's the difference? The public won't yell, because they don't know the difference between a good case and a rotten case, and in another day or two the judge will throw the whole thing out of court, and Eve Mackenzie gets a million dollars worth of publicity, which ain't bad for a washed-up movie star, and we close our file and that's the end of it."

"And the killer walks away, and we never even know *who* he killed or where the real Mackenzie is, if there is a real Mackenzie."

"You been sniffing around."

"That's what I get paid for."

Wainwright got up and stalked around his desk and stood staring out the window. "Times I hate this place and times I love it, and times the goddamn sunshine makes me sick. Look, Masao, this is tied into the Fenwick Works and a lot of other things. They come to me and they tell me to close the book on the Mackenzie case. Indict the wife and then let the case fall apart. She walks out of court free, and that's the end of it. I tell them we don't do things that way."

"Who?"

"There's no who. I gave my word about it. Then they start turning the screw. They put the heat on the city manager, and then the calls come in from Washington, and then more heat—and all along the rationale is that nobody hurts. They want to bury the case. They want an unhappy wife who gets rid of her husband, only there's no good evidence to convict her. Baxter thinks he's going to testify, but Geffner will forget to call him."

"But why? What's behind all this? You tell me that Geffner's in on it, but Geffner's honest."

"We're all honest."

"Is the judge in on it too?"

"Don't put me in the middle of some lousy conspiracy. If we had one small notion of who the real killer is, it would be a different ball game."

"And you don't? Not even one small notion?"

"I want you to stay out of this, Masao. It's done with."

"You know it's a beauty, Captain. For some reason Eve Mackenzie knows what she shouldn't know, so they frame a case around her and put their own lawyers in to defend her, and tell her that she takes her choice—keep her mouth shut and walk out of there a free woman or talk and sit in jail for ten years. Only it's so damn stupid it has to fall apart. What happens then?"

"We're cops. We don't make laws and we don't run the country. We're just cops."

"Sure."

"And now, suppose you get out of here. Lunch is over. I got work to do."

"Would you mind if I looked around the Mackenzie house?"

"I sure as hell would mind. Stay out of there."

Angry, puzzled, and to a degree bewildered, Masuto returned to his car and drove down Lexington Road to the Mackenzie house. He parked his aging Datsun across the street from the big, expensive house, a two-story brick painted white, with a tile roof and high walls on either side to hide the grounds behind the house, and to the left of the house a gated driveway. While Masuto sat there the front door opened and a woman stepped out, a tall, well-built lady of about forty, her hair dark, her figure a bit heavy but still attractive. She stared directly at Masuto for a minute or so, and then she went back into the house.

A few minutes later a Beverly Hills prowl car pulled up alongside Masuto, and the officer driving said, "I didn't know it was you, Sergeant. The lady in the house called in a suspicious car. You got to admit that Datsun of yours is pretty suspicious in the neighborhood."

"I guess it is," Masuto admitted.

He drove back to the police station, studied the blotter, and found nothing to interest him. Sensible professional criminals, with some exceptions, steered shy of Beverly Hills. It was too heavily policed. Burglaries, house break-ins for the most part, were done by amateurs or kids. Car thefts led the list. Masuto was staring at the list without actually seeing it when Wainwright entered his office.

"When Beckman finishes at court," Wainwright said, "he'll fill you in on the follow-ups. Today, you might as well knock off."

"I want to talk to Geffner."

"That's your affair, Masao. Do it on your own time."

Masuto drove back to Santa Monica and got into the crowded courtroom by flashing his badge. Beckman was still on the stand, being cross-examined by Cassell.

"And you actually believe," Cassell was saying to him, "that this woman, Eve Mackenzie, who weighs a hundred and fourteen pounds, could bend over her husband while he sat in the tub and knock him unconscious? Come on, Detective Beckman."

"If she used a hammer—" Beckman began.

Geffner interrupted with an objection. "The question calls for a conclusion," he said. "Detective Beckman is not a physician."

"I'm going to allow it," Judge Simpkins said. "I must say that I'm not thrilled by any of the evidence you've presented thus far, Mr. Geffner, and with this witness you've opened every door imaginable. Don't ask me to close them. Anyway, it's almost five o'clock. I think we'll adjourn."

Beckman spotted Masuto and joined him, and Masuto told him that he intended to talk to Geffner and that it wouldn't be possible if Geffner's star witness listened in.

"This is one time I wish I could." Beckman sighed. "It's been a long, stupid day. I'll see you tomorrow."

Geffner was surrounded by reporters, and Masuto waited until he had worked his way out of them. Then Masuto fell in next to him as Geffner walked out of the courthouse, and Geffner said, "So you're back, Masuto. I wish you had been here. This mess might have been less messy."

"Not likely. I have to talk to you."

"That can only mean grief. I have enough grief."

"You can't make the grief go away, and at least I don't print what I hear."

"All right. I'll meet you at the bar of the Seaview, Ocean Avenue just off Wilshire."

"I know the place."

In the dark comfort of the bar at the Seaview, slumped in a heavy carved wood and black leather chair out of another era, Geffner said, "Masuto, I've practiced law for twenty-five years, and this is the first dirty trick I've ever been caught up in, and so help me God, I can't make head or tail of it, and I don't know whether I'm being honest or dishonest or what."

"I think you should talk about it," Masuto said.

"You know something, I'm going to, because if I don't talk to someone about this, I'll go out of my mind. Beckman was the arresting officer, but the file came to me via Wainwright. Very curious. I told him that there simply wasn't enough clean evidence to go into a preliminary hearing with, that it wouldn't wash. He just shrugged it off and he tells me I got to, you got to. I said no, no judge would move to indict. Then I get a call from Washington. Not direct. First Senator Haitman calls. I know him. I know his voice. He tells me a very important top-secret call from Washington is coming in. Who? What? Nothing but innuendo. Then the call comes. From the White House. Not the President. Gives me an extension and tells me to call back. I call back. This is the White House, she says. I give her the extension and the guy tells me to take the Mackenzie case and see it through. I tell him it's a rotten, tainted case. You take it and see it through, he tells me. I argue that any sane judge will dump it at the preliminary. Just present it, he tells me, if they dump, they dump."

"And you don't know who he is—this voice?"

"Not a glimmer. But the preliminary hearing was before Judge Speeker. He's crazy as a bedbug on the film business. Hates it. The film people ruined California, according to him. He gives us our indictment. So there I am scheduled to go into court without enough evidence to convict this lady of robbing a gumball machine. Well, you saw the beginning. The only other witness I have is that ridiculous Mrs. Scott. I can't put Baxter on. He'd blow the whole thing."

"Eve Mackenzie—she's out on bail?"

"A hundred thousand—very low for murder one. The Fenwick outfit put up the bail."

"And the lawyers were from the same place?"

"Exactly."

"Gets stranger and stranger. What will you do?"

"Finish my case. If Cassell doesn't make a motion—well, he has to make a motion to dismiss, and that's the end of it."

"The judge dismisses, and she walks out free."

"That's about what it adds up to. I suppose Wainwright closes the book then. But to what end, Masuto? That's what drives me crazy. A man who works for Fenwick is killed. Everyone—Washington, Fenwick, your bunch there in Beverly Hills—everyone wants his wife charged with the murder. But they know there's no evidence. They know she'll walk out. Why?"

"That's quite a question."

"Obviously, someone read the notebook and framed the lady. My candidate is Feona Scott." He ordered a second double Scotch. "Who ever heard of a name like that?"

"British. Scottish."

"She's attractive until you see the eyes. Gimlet eyes. Mackenzie says it's not her husband. Mackenzie. I mean Eve, Mrs. Mackenzie, she says it's not her husband."

"Maybe not. Tell me, do you know who her agent is?"

"Eve Mackenzie? I don't even know whether she has one. She hasn't done any films lately."

"Ah, so. What's your guess about Washington?"

"That's it. It makes no sense. Even if Mackenzie was involved in some super-secret stuff, why prosecute his wife without evidence? Unless they felt that in this way the real killer would be protected. But how? And who's the killer? Feona Scott? How about that?"

Masuto shook his head.

"I wish I were defending the lady," Geffner said moodily. "I'd tear the state's case to shreds. I'd be another F. Lee Bailey. You know, in England that's the way it works. Lawyers switch from the prosecution to the defense and back again. Makes more sense than the way we do it. Well, what do you intend to do about all this, Masuto?"

"I work for the city. That doesn't leave me much choice. I argued with Wainwright, but I guess the same voice from Washington convinced him to close the book. He won't reopen the case. Unless—"

"Unless what?"

"Just a notion, but unlikely. One more thing. Did you talk to Eve Mackenzie?"

"The formal stuff. I asked her whether she wanted to plead. She smiled at me and said, 'No, Mr. Geffner, we must have a trial.' "

"She wasn't disturbed?"

"Not a bit. Cool as a cucumber."

Masuto paid the check. "I'll be off now. Thank you."

"Thank you for nothing," Geffner said.

6

What Masuto's wife, Kati, disliked most about those times when he would become totally engrossed with a case was his habit of withdrawal; and this evening, when he returned to his cottage in Culver City after talking with Geffner, it was immediately apparent. He answered questions with monosyllables and he listened without hearing. Kati had once mentioned to him on such an occasion that his Zen Roshi in downtown Los Angeles might not respond well to someone who listened without hearing. It was very un-Japanese on the part of Kati, but since she had become part of a Nisei consciousness-raising group, she did a number of things that were un-Japanese.

When they were in Japan, Kati had been less impressed than Masuto by the food, holding that her mother's cooking was better. She also thought that her own cooking was in most cases superior, but that was a thought she would never voice. However, tonight she had prepared a complex and unusual dinner, a little bit of tuna sushi to begin, then suimono, a delicious soup flavored with ginger and dashi, and then oyako domburi, a chicken dish that takes long and patient preparation. When her husband ate without commenting, Kati said, "If I were an Anglo lady, I would be very angry. I might even shout and scream at you. I might even leave you."

"Kati, what on earth are you talking about?"

"About what your Roshi would say if you spoke to him without hearing what he said."

"Kati, you're making no sense."

"You've eaten the sushi and the suimono. Now you are eating oyako domburi."

"Of course."

"But no comment. Is it good, bad, indifferent? Better than what we ate in Tokyo? Worse? You never even noticed what you were eating."

"Of course I did. Delicious."

"You're just saying that."

"I say it and I mean it. And I appreciate it."

"What did you have for lunch?"

He took refuge in an outright lie. "Hamburgers," he said.

She was mollified. "How can you eat such food! I'm a thoughtless wife. I should pack a lunch basket for you. But I become jealous and thoughtless when you have one of those dreadful murders, and at first I was so happy that we were in Japan when it happened, but now I can see that it waited for you."

"Well, I work in Beverly Hills, Kati. You must know how I feel."

"I think murder is awful, but when a woman kills someone, it's so much worse."

"You mean Eve Mackenzie?"

"Yes."

"She didn't kill her husband, Kati."

"How do you know that? Because she's so pretty?"

Masuto leaned back. "The dinner was wonderful, Kati, and I love you, and the children are in bed, and I'm so glad to be home in our own house. I'm thirsty too, so I'd love a pot of tea and some cake. I know I don't talk much about my cases, but I want to talk about this one and see if I can straighten some of it out in my own mind. Would you like that?"

Kati smiled and nodded, and Masuto felt that he had made up in some degree for his boorishness about the food. Kati was quite right about his not listening. In another person it might be forgivable; in him it was not. Kati poured the tea and sat facing him, and once again he reminded himself that his wife was a truly lovely woman.

"Will you ask me questions?"

"If you wish me to. You mean when I am confused. I heard on the TV this afternoon that she said the dead man was not her husband. Can you tell me what she meant by that?"

"Exactly. What is apparent everyone sees. What is not apparent is not seen. If a tree is cut down, it's invisible, even though it was there before."

"Now if you begin that kind of Zen talk that always confuses me—"

"No. I promise you, although in a way what is happening here is very Zen. It's the work of an illusionist, but not a very bright one, I think.

You asked me about Eve Mackenzie's husband. No, she did not kill him. I'm quite sure she killed no one, but specifically not her husband."

"But the dead man?"

"Not her husband."

"She wasn't married? That's what the man on television said, that the only explanation for Mrs. Mackenzie's statement was that they had never been married."

"Hardly. And if he weren't lazy and had checked some records, he would have discovered that Mr. and Mrs. Mackenzie were married."

"But the dead man?"

"He was not her husband because he was not Robert Mackenzie. A number of other people identified him as Mackenzie, but that was because they had seen Mackenzie only with his clothes on. His wife had seen him naked, and when she looked at the body in the tub she saw something that was missing, and as I said before, what is missing is invisible."

"Ah, so—yes!" Kati exclaimed. "An operation scar, a birthmark, of course. Then who is the dead man?"

"Who do you think he is, Kati?"

"Only one person can look so alike. It's Mr. Mackenzie's twin brother."

"Good!" Masuto said with pleasure. "Again, Kati, the apparent and the unapparent. When Mrs. Mackenzie said that the man was not her husband they put it down to the unreliability of a woman's mind or witness. If one has contempt for women, then one puts no stock in a woman's statement."

"Yes, yes," Kati agreed. "We were discussing that at our conscious-ness-raising group. And I think, Masao, it's even worse among Nisei women—"

"Perhaps."

"I didn't mean you, Masao," Kati said apologetically.

"You must. I'm as bad an offender as any. But you do see the position of Mrs. Mackenzie. She declares the dead man is not her husband. A dozen men swear that she is mistaken. The dead man is her husband. But can a woman be mistaken on such a question? Hardly, and since all the male witnesses plus Mrs. Scott insist that the dead man is Robert Mackenzie, it is accepted and Mrs. Mackenzie is arrested."

"Then she did not kill her husband. Did she kill his twin brother? Why did his clothes have to disappear? I don't understand that," Kati said.

"He was found naked in the bathtub. Why? Why did he have to be sitting naked in the tub unless to provide a reason for his clothes to disappear. There are a hundred ways to kill a man. Why go to something so exotic as an electrocution in a bathtub?"

"But that was in her notebook."

"Yes, which meant that the media and the police and everyone else would be looking at the notebook instead of wondering where the dead man's clothes had gotten to."

Kati shook her head. "I don't understand, Masao."

"No? Of course, it's murky. It's the kind of thing that fills one with a sense of foreboding and horror. But let me reconstruct it as a playwright might to put together a scene. Mackenzie has a twin brother. The twin brother appears and must be killed."

"Why?"

"I don't know that. Kati, I know none of this, and I try to spin something out of invisible cloth. So I invent a twin brother who must be killed. Since he was killed, I presume that he must be killed. Since he was found naked, I presume that his clothes must be disposed of. He was knocked unconscious by a blow to the head. Now he lies unconscious. Two choices: dispose of the body, dispose of the clothes. Which choice? It's not easy to make a body vanish—easier to make the clothes vanish."

Kati shuddered. "How can you live with this, Masao? Day and night."

"It's my karma."

Kati shook her head.

"No more?"

"Yes," Kati said. "Please go on. Does it help? I mean for me to listen and ask questions."

"A great deal."

"Yes—the choice is to make the clothes vanish. But why? Why must the body be naked? Ah, so!" he exclaimed. "I am as witless as the others."

"Why?"

"One or two of three people are present at the murder. Perhaps others, but certainly one or more of three. Because there are three people who presumably knew the contents of Eve Mackenzie's notebook."

"Yes, yes," Kati agreed excitedly. "Her husband, Mrs. Scott, and Mrs. Mackenzie. That's why they arrested Mrs. Mackenzie. But why couldn't they arrest the other two?"

"Kati, Kati, the presumption was that Mr. Mackenzie was dead. And Mrs. Scott had no motive, and she told of a terrible fight between the Mackenzies. I'm sure that if the trial lasts long enough to put Mrs. Scott on the stand, she will testify that Mrs. Mackenzie threatened to kill her husband."

"But you don't think she killed him?"

"Oh, no. Mrs. Mackenzie is a small, slender woman. She can't weigh more than a hundred and ten or fifteen pounds. According to Sy Beckman, the man in the tub weighed at least two hundred pounds. Mrs. Mackenzie could never place his body in the tub."

"But Mrs. Scott?"

"Stronger, a very well-built woman. No, I don't think so, and that leaves Mackenzie as the murderer of his twin brother. Or does it? Any number of different people could have been there. We have no motive. It's not a random killing, not a burglary, not some lunatic lying up in the hills and shooting at cars on the freeway. No, indeed. This is murder with malice aforethought. But why? And why did Eve Mackenzie suddenly stop insisting that the man in the tub was not her husband?"

"Until the trial," Kati said.

"But why the trial? Why did she subject herself to the trial? You see, Kati, the state's case was built on the fact that Mackenzie was taking a bath when his wife struck him with a blunt instrument and then executed him. But if it turned out not to be Mackenzie, then he would not be calmly bathing in Mackenzie's bathtub and there would be absolutely no case against Mrs. Mackenzie. And why the refusal to give Beckman Mackenzie's fingerprints? Senseless, stupid—and horrible."

"Murder is always horrible."

"Yes—" It flickered in his mind. It was a picture unreal, like a television screen out of focus, waving, the sought-for images mixed with images unsought. He had called himself witless, and properly as he thought about it now. Eve Mackenzie had been dealt into whatever game was being played here. A deal had been made with her agreement. That's why she stood trial with such aplomb, and that's why her bail had been no more than a hundred thousand dollars, paid for by the Fenwick company, even as Fenwick had supplied her legal defense. The Fenwick Works, Mackenzie, his twin brother, Eve Mackenzie, a trial that was ridiculous and would be thrown out of court and then the book closed. But why the trial?

"They wanted the trial—" Masuto began.

"Who, Masao?"

"Just listen to me, Kati, and let me say it aloud and try to have it make sense. Eve Mackenzie hates her husband. She wants a divorce. He will not give her a divorce. There could be any number of reasons for that. They have a fight, not unusual, and she drives to Santa Barbara to spend the night with her sister. That night, Mackenzie's twin shows up. Possibly, Mackenzie is not alone. He or they kill the twin. Maybe Scott is in on it, maybe not. What to do with the body? Notebook—frame Eve Mackenzie. But something is missing from the twin, a birthmark or operation scar. That gives Eve the upper hand. She will play ball for a price."

"What price could justify her lying to cover up for a murder?"

"My dear Kati, all women are not like you. She might have desired to divorce so desperately she would tell any lie to get it. She may want money. What do we know about her—or about any film star? The image we see on the screen is not the person."

"Masao?"

"Yes?"

"May I be permitted a doubt?"

Masuto smiled and nodded.

"Of course it was on the news today. She said that the dead man was not her husband. She did not keep a promise of silence. Then what happened to the deal you say she made?"

"I don't know. She might have been frightened, she might have felt that the others would double-cross her. Perhaps she feels it is time to look after herself."

"None of it makes sense to me," Kati said. "Does it make sense to you, Masao?"

"No, not much."

"And if the case is dismissed, as you say, if it's thrown out of court, will you go on looking for the murderer?"

"I don't know. That's up to Captain Wainwright, and my guess is that he doesn't know either."

"I must do the dishes," Kati said. "I feel that I have been with you into one of those horrible investigations, but still I must do the dishes."

7

Masuto bathed, put on his saffron terry-cloth robe, and went into the tiny sun room at the back of his cottage which he somewhat abashedly called his meditation room. There was on the floor only a mat and a small round pillow. Masuto had found that even a half hour of Zen meditation cleared his mind and renewed his body. But tonight he was not to have a half hour of meditation. He had been sitting there for only minutes when he heard the doorbell ring. The house was small, and the hearing of a meditating person is very keen, and to his astonishment, Masuto heard the voice of Geffner, the district attorney, asking for him.

"You come at an unfortunate time," Kati protested.

"It's all right," Masuto called out. "Put Mr. Geffner in the living room. I'll be right there."

Masuto put on his street clothes before he went into the living room. It would embarrass Geffner to face him with a saffron robe, and Geffner was embarrassed enough. "It's almost eleven o'clock," he said to Masuto, "and I just can't tell you how awkward I feel about barging in here like this. But I had to see you, Masuto, and it was on my way."

"On your way?" Masuto asked, puzzled. "The court is in Santa Monica and you live in Encino, so how can Culver City be on your way?"

"I was downtown, Masuto. The judge asked me to come to his chambers down there. He's going to throw out the case tomorrow. I agree with him. But then, while I was there, we got the news that Eve Mackenzie is dead."

"What? No—Eve Mackenzie?"

Geffner nodded.

"I've been a fool—a total, stupid fool!" Masuto exclaimed. "A woman is dead. She was murdered."

"Oh?" Geffner stared at him. "Why do you say that?"

"How did she die?"

"A car accident."

"Where?"

Geffner stared at him thoughtfully. "Why murder?"

"First tell me where she died and how."

"Malibu Canyon. You know the road—one of the most dangerous in the county. The story is that she was driving too fast and she went over the edge, through the guardrail, and into a seventy-foot ravine."

"Whose story? Who did you talk to?"

"The California Highway Patrol."

"Mental giants."

"Masuto, they're pretty good with accidents."

"Then why are you here?"

"Because I think what you're thinking—that it was no accident."

"And you ask me why I think so?" Masuto said angrily. "This is the most idiotic frame and contrivance I have ever heard of. And you lent yourself to it, and now the woman is dead. Of course I said murder. The moment she blurted out that the man in the tub was not her husband, she was doomed."

"Don't come down on me, Masuto. I didn't lend myself to it. I was told what to do, and at that point I didn't know what was valid evidence and what was not."

Masuto nodded. "Sorry. I should not have said that. Tell me, what was Eve Mackenzie doing at night on the Malibu Canyon Road?"

"I don't know. I would guess she was at the Fenwick Works. That appears to be the source of everything in this insane case. I want you to come with me to Malibu Canyon tonight, Masuto. I want to look at the wreck, and I want you with me."

"You can't be serious. I'm a Beverly Hills policeman. The accident belongs to the highway patrol, and they're there already. If there's any suggestion of criminal action, they'll turn to the Malibu Sheriff's Station. The sheriffs are not very nice people to begin with, and if they see a Beverly Hills cop putting his nose into things, they'll skin me."

"It's in the county and I have jurisdiction," Geffner said, "and if they can prove I haven't, we'll be out of there before they find the right page in the book. I won't introduce you as a Beverly Hills cop. Joe Hendricks is waiting outside in my car. He's the L.A.P.D. accident consultant, and I'll introduce you as his assistant."

"I work for a living," Masuto said. "All I know is being a cop and growing roses. If Wainwright hears about this—"

"Damn it, Masuto, you're doing nothing wrong. I'm asking for your help as a private citizen."

Masuto sighed. "All right. Wait for me outside. I'll talk to my wife."

But Kati did nothing to soften Masuto's doubts. "I didn't want to listen, Masao," she said, "but in this house you can't help overhearing. It's eleven o'clock, and you're doing something that isn't right, and I won't sleep—"

"What I'm doing is perfectly all right."

"Is it? The story you told me tonight makes me terribly afraid."

Masuto understood that. There was a thread of madness running through it that would make any normal person afraid.

8

Hendricks was a large, overweight man with the broad, heavy hands and splayed fingers of a garage mechanic. As a matter of fact, he had been a mechanic a good part of his life, and there was, as Geffner put it, nothing about cars that he did not know.

"I don't buy the perfect murder," he said to Masuto as they drove north on the Pacific Coast Highway. "I don't buy it at all. You fix a car and somewhere it's got to show. You cut a brake line, it shows. You fix the wheel, it shows."

"But suppose you do nothing to the car," Masuto insisted. "You knock out a person and put her behind the wheel. Do it on a downhill stretch in a place like Malibu Canyon. She goes through the guardrail. What then?"

"Suppose the car burns," Geffner said.

"Sure, those things can happen, but mostly they don't. Every time you turn on the television you see a car go out of control and burst into flames. You ever see a car in a highway crash burst into flame?"

"Once or twice," Masuto said. "I didn't actually see it happen, but I was called in."

"Never saw it myself," Geffner admitted.

"Tell you how they do it, Mr. Geffner. They use a small incendiary charge. Sometimes they blow it by remote control, sometimes it's set to go off on contact."

"The car didn't burn. I didn't talk to the highway patrol myself. Evidently, they phoned it in to the county sheriff in Hollywood and he called Judge Simpkins. I guess he felt that Simpkins ought to know as soon as possible."

"What about the media?" Masuto asked.

"We'll know when we get there. I hope we get there first."

"What are you going to tell the highway cops?" Masuto asked.

"We'll see what they tell us. The highway patrol likes to feel that they own the state. It's not exactly the truth."

At the Malibu Colony, Geffner made a right turn off the Pacific Coast Highway and into the hills. Driving that way, they could see the night lights of the Fenwick Works, built on a low hill and facing the Pacific, a great, sprawling complex of buildings, with a lit sign that said: TOMORROW IS TODAY AT FENWICK. The Malibu Canyon Road ran eastward, connecting the Pacific coast with the San Fernando Valley, and in the course of its ten-mile journey from the coast to the Valley, it ran through some of the most splendidly scenic country in the West. While not unusually high, the mountains that bordered the road were precipitous, shelves of raw rock that climbed a thousand and fifteen hundred feet from a road frequently gouged out of the rock itself. Daytime, the road was as beautiful as it was dangerous; at night, it was simply dangerous.

They had come over thirty miles from Culver City, and Masuto wondered what compelled a district attorney who, at best, could only claim to have lost a comely defendant.

"No," Geffner said. "I've been had. The state's been had. It stinks. Someone is playing dirty games, and for them the law means nothing and the court means nothing. Maybe I simply want to validate the way I earn a living."

"It's not easy," Masuto said. "I've tried."

There were lights up ahead, enough light to make a glow over the road, and then there were the cars lined up on the narrow shoulder, CBS News and ABC News and NBC News and the press cars and the independent TV stations and some traffic and a tow truck trying to get through, and two long, sleek black limousines which, Masuto guessed, might be the property of Fenwick Works, and, their lights flashing, two highway patrol cars and a sheriff's car out of Malibu Station. It was a large company, but the violent death of a star is not an everyday occurrence, and the death of a star on trial for murder is worth everything the media can give it, and the media would certainly give it Masao Masuto among other things. Masuto felt that he should have realized this before he ever allowed Geffner to lure him out of his meditation chamber.

They squeezed onto the shoulder behind the two black limousines. The windows of the limousines, darkened glass, were quite opaque. The chauffeurs, men with hard, expressionless faces, stood by their cars. Masuto made a mental note of the license plate of the car in front of them. Masuto, Geffner, and Hendricks got out of their car and walked down the road to where a lieutenant in the highway patrol stood center-stage to a circle of news and television people.

"I know him," Masuto told Geffner. "The lieutenant. That's Archie Delt. Not the sweetest man in the world. He'll be sore as hell to see a Beverly Hills cop out here in Malibu."

"The hell with him!"

"I'll hold that thought," Masuto said wryly.

The tow truck was trying to maneuver into a position near the break in the guardrail where it might drop a hook from its winch, and Masuto wondered why the haste to bring up the wrecked car, since the woman's body had been removed. Another part of his mind was following the questions and answers—questions thrown by the TV people and reporters.

"Who pronounced her dead?" a reporter asked. "Was there a doctor on the scene?"

"Patrolman Gilbert climbed down to the car. It was not entirely dark. As I said before, Mrs. Mackenzie's neck was broken. She had numerous other injuries and she had no pulse. Then Patrolman Anderson arrived on the scene and the two of them managed to remove Mrs. Mackenzie from the car and carry her up to the road."

"Why was she sent to All Saints Hospital? Why not to a local hospital?"

Lieutenant Delt was patient with the questions, even though they tended to be repetitive. He was not unaware of the TV cameras fixed on him as he stood in the glare of the emergency lights.

"If Mrs. Mackenzie had not been dead, she would have been rushed immediately to the nearest hospital. But she was dead and had been dead for at least an hour before we brought her body up to the road. She was taken to All Saints because that's the Beverly Hills hospital and that's where her physician instructed us to take the body and she is a resident of Beverly Hills. Does that answer your question?"

Delt finally excused himself. The tow truck was in place, and the emergency lights were turned on the canyon. The car could be seen now, a small, two-seater Mercedes, apparently not too damaged. The press was drifting away. Masuto noticed two men in civilian clothes in whispered conference with Delt, and one of them glanced at him and then nudged Delt and whispered to him. Delt walked over to where

Hendricks, Geffner, and Masuto were standing. Meanwhile, the tow truck crew were feeding the cable down into the ravine.

"Far from home, Sergeant," Delt said to Masuto. "You didn't just happen to be driving through the canyon?"

"I'm afraid not," Masuto said. "We heard that a very unlikely thing had happened here, and District Attorney Geffner and—"

Geffner nodded slightly.

"—and Officer Hendricks of the Los Angeles police and myself— well, we'd like to look at the car when they bring it up."

"It would appear to me," Delt said, "that you're all a little outside of your jurisdiction."

"Just hold on," Geffner said coldly. "This is L.A. County, so don't read me any lessons on jurisdiction. The dead woman was arrested and charged in Beverly Hills, and as far as Officer Hendricks is concerned, he's here as an assisting officer, courtesy of L.A.P.D., and his specialty is car crime, and I want him to look at Eve Mackenzie's car. Any objections?"

During this the two men who had been talking to Delt moved up to join the little circle, and one of them, a tall, well-built handsome man of about sixty years, with white hair and cold blue eyes, said quickly and firmly, "Of course we have no objection. On the contrary, I'm certain Lieutenant Delt is as delighted as we are. If there have been any dirty tricks around this awful accident, we are more eager than anyone to clear them up."

Delt was silent, and Geffner asked, "Who are you, sir, and who are the we?"

"I'm Alan Soames. I'm general manager at the Fenwick Works." And nodding to his companion, "This is Mr. Slocum. And if you're curious about why we're here, well, the highway patrol informed us immediately."

"Was Mrs. Mackenzie with you this evening?"

"I'm afraid so. Tragically. Otherwise she might not have been driving through the canyon and this awful thing might never have happened."

"Could I ask what she was doing at the Fenwick Works?" Masuto said.

"No, I don't think so, Sergeant—what did you say your name was?"

"Masuto."

"Masuto? Japanese—or as you say, Nisei. You're a policeman?"

"I'm afraid so. My name is Masao Masuto, Beverly Hills police force. And just for the record, Mr. Soames, may I have it that you refuse to answer any questions regarding Eve Mackenzie's reasons for being at your plant and driving home through the canyon?"

"No, you may not. You've twisted my words out of shape, and I don't like that, Masuto, not one bit. I did not say I refuse to answer questions. No, sir! I simply said that I deny your right to ask them."

"Ah, so. Very plain."

With that Soames turned on his heel and walked off, followed by Slocum, who remained unidentified. Delt stared at Geffner and Masuto, his hands on his hips. "What is it you want?" he asked them. "Another murder? Someone tampered with her car and dumped her over the cliff? Or is it just that the California Highway Patrol is too damn stupid to know which side is up—until a Beverly Hills cop decides to tell us?"

"Come on, Lieutenant," Masuto said softly. "We have no vendetta going, so let's not start one. Soames will get into his big limo back there and go off to wherever such people go. You and I, we remain cops. I need a favor, you need a favor."

"Okay, we'll cool it. But how the hell would you feel if we walked into Beverly Hills and told you that you didn't know what the hell you were doing."

"Mostly we don't." Masuto grinned. "So any time you feel like, come by. I'll welcome you with open arms."

"Bullshit."

"So what do you think?" Masuto asked him. "That little Mercedes down there is one of the best cars in the world. Why did she go through the guardrail?"

"Because the best cars in the world are no better than who drives them. Maybe she was loaded."

"Will there be an autopsy?"

"Masuto, I can't ask for an autopsy until I have some indication that a crime was committed. You know that."

"But her family can," Geffner said. "She has a sister in Santa Barbara."

"That's up to them." Delt turned to Hendricks. "Are you really good with car accidents?"

"So they say."

"All right." And to Masuto, softly, "I don't like being pushed around any more than you do, and I don't work for Soames or Fenwick and I don't like being told what to do and what not to do. I wasn't going to stand between you and that car wreck. Hendricks can go over it with a fine-tooth comb, and if he finds something, then sure as hell it was done between here and the Fenwick Works."

But Hendricks found nothing—at least nothing in the way of mechanical manipulation of the car. He spent almost an hour going over every inch of it, and he found no severed brake lines, no steering wheel tampering, no loosened wheels—none of a half dozen other possibilities. Nothing that was done, only something that was not done.

"What was that?" Delt asked him.

"She was not wearing her seat belt."

"How do you know?"

"On this model Mercedes, there's no automatic return."

"What does that say?"

"Well, look at the car," Hendricks said. "This happens once in a while. It hit the guardrail and popped that log right off, which shows how much that guardrail was worth. But the car was hardly damaged from that blow. Then it went right down that face with no obstruction at all until it hit the mesquite, and then the mesquite cushioned it. The steering wheel is still on its mount. If that lady in the car, even without her seat belt, had hung on to the wheel, she could have come through it with no more than a bad scare."

"What are you getting at?" Delt asked him.

"What do you think, Lieutenant? There was nothing wrong with the car. That little car drives like a dream. So why'd she go through the guardrail?"

"Drugged," Masuto said.

"Or drunk."

"They couldn't be sure there won't be an autopsy. So it would be something simple," Masuto said. "Something she could have used herself."

"Who are *they*?" Delt asked him. "And with that scenario, why didn't her head go through the windshield?"

They turned to Hendricks, who said, "It wouldn't necessarily. She might have fallen over on the seat while still up here on the road. Then her head would hit the dashboard, where there's a good deal of blood. Look at it yourselves."

There was blood all over the car seat and the dashboard. Delt pressed Masuto. "You're so goddamn sure she was murdered. They did this and they did that. Who?"

Masuto shook his head. "It's a presumption, that's all." There was a lot that Geffner might have said, but Masuto could appreciate the position of a district attorney who had been prosecuting a case that was no case, only to have his suspect killed. There were still a couple of reporters hanging around and a photographer from the *L.A. Times* was snapping pictures of the wrecked car. Anything Geffner said could be flushed back in his face. A D.A. who allows himself to be persuaded by pressure from Washington to take a stupid case that won't hold is in no position to court publicity.

Delt's face was blank.

"A very good and sound presumption, I think," Masuto said. "You know what the situation is out here in the canyon, Lieutenant. It's an unincorporated area, and if you drop that line of inquiry, the Malibu sheriff's office sure as hell is not going to pick it up."

"What's it to you, Masuto? Just tell me what's in it for you that you got to push like this. You're a Beverly Hills cop and you're thirty miles from home. The woman's dead."

It was not easy to explain, and Masuto was not even certain that he could explain. One's work took over, the man became the work, and the work became the man. That was not anything Delt would comprehend.

"She lived in a town I'm supposed to protect."

"That's a load, Masuto, and you know it. I can see Mr. Geffner's point. He's involved. But the way I look at it, you're not involved. Don't put down the sheriff's deputies out here in Malibu. They ain't totally brainless. I never seen a city cop didn't think the country boy was a working moron."

"Time I was getting back home," Hendricks said.

"Time we all were," Geffner agreed. His glance at Masuto said to keep the situation in low key. No use turning Delt into an enemy.

Masuto nodded. "Things come back home. I'll return the favor one day, Lieutenant."

"You've been damn cooperative. I'll remember," Geffner said.

Delt shook hands with the district attorney. "Almost two in the morning," he said. "I get frayed around the edges when these things push away a man's sleep. You figure you've seen everything and nothing gets to you, but I watched her movies when I was a kid and to see her pulled out of that car like a smashed, bloody bundle of rags was not nice."

"I can understand that," Masuto agreed.

"Okay, Sergeant. See you at the races."

They walked back up the road to where the car was parked. Aside from the police cars, only a few autos were still parked alongside the road. The two big limousines had departed. Hendricks got into the backseat, leaving the front seat next to the driver for Masuto.

"I'll go on down into the Valley," Geffner told them. "Ventura Freeway and then the San Diego Freeway. It's the quickest way and it takes us right through Culver City. You'll be home by two-thirty," he said to Masuto. "That's not too bad."

"No, not bad at all. I'm glad you played it straight with Delt. I don't love him, but he's an honest cop."

"We're all honest," Geffner said. "That's what beats the hell out of me. If we were crooks or takers or on some kind of a pad, we wouldn't be here in the canyon at a quarter to two in the morning trying to make sense out of something that makes no sense. My mother calls me every day. Tomorrow she'll call me and ask me where I was last night, and then I'll try to explain to her why I'm here. Only—"

He had pulled out into the road and started down toward the Valley, his lights on, picking up speed on the straight downward stretch after the curve where the car went through the guardrail, and now suddenly he broke off what he was saying. There was a long moment of silence.

"Hendricks?"

"Yes, sir."

"I have no brakes."

The car was picking up speed.

"The hand brake! Slow, even pressure."

The hand brake was between the front seats. Masuto eased it back and said, "No hand brake!"

"Now, listen," Hendricks said quickly. "Into the left lane, Mr. Geffner, and lay the car up against the cliff. Now! But easy, easy, just shave the paint."

On the right, the canyon dropped away, fifty, a hundred feet; on their left, the canyon wall rose up above them. They were doing almost fifty miles an hour as Geffner moved into the left lane and let the car touch the canyon wall. The screeching, grinding sound of metal bent and torn by the rock sidewall brought forth a moan of despair from Geffner. The car jerked and rocked under the continuing impact, but the speed was cut, and Hendricks shouted above the noise, "Hang on, Mr. Geffner! I want you to put her into reverse. Do it quickly with a snap motion, and then brace yourself."

"You're going to destroy my car!" Geffner wailed.

"But we'll live to see it done. Now, Sergeant!"

Masuto drove the automatic shift handle into reverse, and the car shuddered to the tearing sound of stripped gears and then came to a stop against the cliff face, the radiator steaming and, behind it, for almost a mile up the road, a trail or torn parts—mirrors, a fender, the rear bumper, the rear left door, bits and pieces of assorted glass and metal. For a long moment the three men sat in silence, not moving.

Then Hendricks drew a deep breath and said, "We'd better get out of the car."

"What's left of it."

"Can it be repaired?" he asked Hendricks.

"No, it's totaled." He pointed back in the darkness. "There—that's a wheel. We lost that just as we were stopping. Torn off the axle. We got out of it just in time. Do you have a flashlight, Mr. Geffner?"

Geffner found a flashlight in his glove compartment and handed it to Hendricks, who crawled under the car.

Shivering, Geffner shook his head. "I don't want him to find what he's looking for."

"It's something we're not used to," Masuto said. "In other countries perhaps, but not here. It's new here. To kill whatever stands in your way, whatever interferes with you. You, me, Hendricks—that's all we have in common. We interfered."

"For God's sake, Sergeant, I've had trouble with the brakes on this car ever since I bought it. Don't invent anything. Don't be imaginative. This is not Iran. This is not El Salvador. We live in a country of law. We've had a bad accident, and we've lived through it."

Hendricks crawled out from under the car. "Somebody doesn't like us," he said wryly.

"What does that mean?"

"It means the brake lines were cut. No foot brake, no hand brake. If it wasn't for your damn brilliant driving, Mr. Geffner, we'd all be nicely dead."

"You're sure?"

"About the brakes? Absolutely."

The night was cold, but not cold enough to account for the chill that went through Masuto.

Geffner had a radiophone in his car, and they put him through to Delt. "We're about a mile or two down the road," Geffner said. "We have problems."

9

It was four o'clock in the morning when Masuto walked into his cottage in Culver City. There had been a time when Kati, worried sick, would have been waiting up for him. Time had forced her to accept the fact that he could be away half the night yet return in one piece. Tonight, or this morning, depending upon one's point of view, Masuto was too tired even for his nightly bath, and in the morning he overslept, missing the time he usually set aside for his meditation. He kissed Kati and fled from the house, and drive as he might, it was still nine-twenty when he reached the police station in Beverly Hills. Since he was expected to clock in at eight-thirty, he was almost an hour late. Polly, at Reception, informed him that the boss was steaming.

He went into the office he shared with Sy Beckman, and Beckman informed him that Wainwright had called his office twice this morning and had appeared in person once—the latter not very difficult since he was directly down the hall.

"What could you have done between yesterday and today?" Beckman wondered. "That kind of burn takes a lot of doing. I see she's dead. What in hell does this case add up to, Masao?"

"Confusion?"

"Poor dame, first that crazy trial and now this."

Captain Wainwright switched to voice contact. Having heard that Masuto was in the building, he stepped into the hall and shouted, "Masuto, get your ass in here!"

Masuto walked down the corridor, nodding to the sympathetic glances of various patrolmen, and went into Wainwright's office. Wainwright was standing there, room center, awaiting him, and for a long moment they stood face to face. Then Wainwright wheeled and took his seat behind his desk.

"Sit down," he told Masuto.

Masuto sat.

"All right. Tell me about it. I try to be a reasonable person. I have been known to get angry at times but with good cause. So just explain it, and let me see it your way."

"Explain?" Masuto smiled. "If I could comprehend and explain anything in this world, I would be an enlightened person, which I am not."

"No, sir." Wainwright's voice dropped. "Don't give me any of that Charlie Chan bullshit, Masao. I want to know what in hell you were doing up in Malibu Canyon last night with Geffner and that high-class grease monkey from the L.A.P.D."

"I can tell you that. Mr. Geffner was disturbed. He appears to have been more or less disturbed since this crazy trial started. Last night, after court, Judge Simpkins told Mr. Geffner that he intended to throw the Mackenzie case out of court the following day. Then Geffner heard that Eve Mackenzie was dead. He suspected murder, and he asked me to drive out to Malibu Canyon with him."

"You're a Beverly Hills cop."

"I'm aware of that."

"Then what in God's name were you doing out there in Malibu Canyon? Whatever happened there, it's out of our jurisdiction."

"Eve Mackenzie was a resident of Beverly Hills."

"And if she was shot in Paris, would you tell that to the Sûreté?"

"Malibu's closer."

"Masao," Wainwright said more gently, "you and me go back a long time and I've cussed you out plenty for bending the rules and maybe breaking them now and then. But I've apologized too, and I've never said that you weren't the smartest cop that ever worked for me. Well, eight o'clock this morning the city manager walks in and he says to me, 'What would you say, Captain, if I told you to fire Masuto?' Just like that."

"What did you say?"

"I asked him what he was doing—was he telling me to fire you, and if so, just why? Or was he just posing the question?"

Masuto waited, smiling slightly.

"No comment?"

"I could go to Hawaii," Masuto said. "I think the children would be happy there, and they don't mind hiring Nisei cops, and if you put the kiss of death on me, I can always work as a security guard or something of the sort—"

"Will you cut out that goddamn crap and be serious for one cotton-picking minute. I told the city manager that if he instructed me to fire you, he could find someone else to run his police department."

"Thank you," Masuto said. "I appreciate that."

"He said he felt the same way. The city manager."

"Then what was it? An exercise in rhetoric?"

"You can bet your sweet life it was not. A guy from the C.I.A. woke him up at two o'clock in the morning—"

"Name of Slocum?"

"I think so, Slocum. Made it important enough to get our city manager out of bed and give him a lecture on what in hell you were doing up in Malibu Canyon in the middle of the night, and this same C.I.A. character informed Abramson that you were impertinent, destructive, and given to dropping dangerous innuendos, and very likely a man engaged in something dirtier than being a cop. Now what in hell gave him that notion, Masao?"

"I might have said that I suspected Eve Mackenzie's death was no accident."

"You had to. You couldn't keep your nose out of it. They have a highway patrol and a sheriff's department, but that don't cut no ice with you. No, sir. You're damn lucky that Abramson doesn't frighten. He told this Slocum guy that the C.I.A. doesn't do the hiring and firing on this police force, and that until he was ready to bring some concrete charges against you, he, Abramson, would take no action. So much for the city manager. Now comes my part of it. Stay out of the Mackenzie case. The book is closed. His wife was charged with the murder, and she's dead. As far as we're concerned, it's over."

"You have to be kidding."

"Like hell I am!"

They sat silently facing each other for about thirty seconds. Then Masuto reached into his pocket, took out his wallet, and opened it to reveal his badge. He unpinned it carefully and placed it on Wainwright's desk. Then he took his gun and placed it on the badge. Then he stood up and said, "So sorry, Captain, so very sorry." He left the office, closing the door gently behind him.

He had taken three steps in the corridor when he was almost physically assaulted by Wainwright's bellow. "Masuto, you get your ass back in here!"

Masuto halted and waited. Doors opened. Heads poked out. Wainwright opened his door and shouted, "You got nothing better to do?" The doors closed. "Masuto, inside!"

Masuto returned to Wainwright's office, closing the door behind him as gently as he had before.

"Sit down!" Wainwright snapped. "What in hell is eating you, Masuto? Haven't I always treated you decently? Didn't I fight to get the first Oriental cop on this force? Haven't I stood behind you and backed you up every time they yelled for your scalp? And then when I get into a situation where I can't back you up, first thing you do is dump your badge and gun and walk out—which is another part of your phony routine," he yelled, thrusting a finger at Masuto, "just like that 'so sorry' crap that you picked up watching the late show—and you got to be the number-one horse's ass to walk out on a job like yours in maybe the best police spot in the country, not to mention our pension plan. So will you pick up your gun and badge, and let's try to talk like two civilized people."

"You're absolutely right about the pension," Masuto said, picking up the gun and badge. "Never thought of it."

"Don't put me on. Just tell me plain and straight why you can't leave this thing alone."

"No, sir. You tell me, Captain, why, when a murder takes place on your turf, you're ready to let the killers walk away scot-free."

"That's not fair, Masao."

"Why not? We both know Eve Mackenzie didn't kill her husband. As a matter of fact, no one killed her husband because the dead man was not her husband. She was pushed into a trial because certain forces wanted it that way, and if I had to guess, I'd guess C.I.A. and Fenwick. And then they murdered her because their whole stupid plan couldn't stand up and they thought she was going to blow the whistle on them, and last night they tried to kill Geffner, Hendricks, and me, and I think that if Hendricks wasn't with us, they might have pulled it off."

"What? Just say that again!"

"They cut the brake lines on Geffner's car while we were looking at the car Eve Mackenzie drove, and it was on a spot just before that long slope in Malibu Canyon, and if you think I'm building up an incident to impress you, call Hendricks down at L.A.P.D. and he'll tell you all about it."

"I don't have to call Hendricks," Wainwright said quietly. "I believe you. Who did it?"

"I don't think there's much question about that. They had two big black limos parked there and a couple of thugs as drivers. That's a guess, but I think it's a damn good guess."

Wainwright sat and stared at his desk. Masuto waited. A clock on Wainwright's desk ticked away the seconds. Finally, Wainwright looked up at Masuto and smiled forlornly. "Well, Masao, we've done some good work together."

"We'll do more."

"Maybe. Only there's a lot of muscle on the other side."

"If they can get away with it here, in this country, kill anyone who stands in their way, manipulate the police, manipulate the courts—well, we let them, don't we? It's our fault. We're the ones who make murder easy—just by keeping our hands off."

"That's right."

"So—what then, Captain? What do we do?"

"A man was murdered in the Mackenzie house. He may have been Mackenzie. Most likely, he was not. When a homicide occurs here in Beverly Hills, it's your responsibility and your department. So I expect you to bring in the killer, and I don't give a damn if the President of the United States calls you down to Washington and stuffs you full of caviar and tells you to lay off. I am sick and tired of being told to keep my nose clean. If Abramson comes down and tells us that we're both fired— well, okay, we'll pack it up. But until then—"

"I'll stir up a lot of garbage. I have to know who killed Eve Mackenzie, if she actually was murdered, and who tried to kill us, and I might have to do some telephoning."

"I don't have to instruct you."

"No, you don't. Thank you, Captain."

"For what?"

Masuto did not say that it took guts and principle to do what Wainwright was doing. Wainwright would not have taken kindly to such a statement.

10

Beckman was waiting for Masuto, and asked him whether he was still working for the Beverly Hills police force. Masuto repeated his conversation with Wainwright, and Beckman wanted to know what it added up to and where it made any sense.

"Mackenzie is killed, or someone who looks enough like him to be his twin brother, and then his wife, and then they go after you and Geffner and Hendricks like they're running a goddamn butcher shop—and why? We don't even have a smell of a motive."

"Just a smell. They wanted Eve Mackenzie dead because she knew too much. But what did she know? She wasn't there when the man in the tub was killed. Did she know who he was? And how does Fenwick figure? Whatever Mackenzie's employment card had on it could have been masked out when they Xeroxed it. So why wouldn't they send you his fingerprints?"

"They knew it wasn't Mackenzie?"

"No question about it. So that wasn't Mackenzie. But why this strange charade? If they wanted to get rid of the twin, why not a shotgun blast in the face. A prowler, and Mackenzie kills him in self-defense. No questions asked, the way people feel today. Mackenzie would come out a sort of hero, and that Fenwick crowd would hardly be disturbed by blowing away a man's face. But instead they work out that ridiculous bathtub murder, as described in Eve's notebook."

"And then they kill her," Beckman said.

"If we can prove it."

"Give it a try, Masao. I know it's outside our turf, but there has to be some way."

Masuto took a deep breath. "All right, first step." He picked up the telephone and called All Saints Hospital. They gave him the pathology room, and a moment later he heard the rasping voice of Dr. Baxter.

"Who? Masuto? Yes, I'll talk to him." And then, on the phone, he snapped, "No, there won't be any autopsy."

"What?"

"You calling about an autopsy for Eve Mackenzie? Well, I got her in the icebox, and there she stays until they make some funeral arrangements."

"Yes, I was going to ask about an autopsy. I thought I'd get over and see you sometime today."

"Save yourself the trip. No crime, no autopsy, unless her sister says so. Her sister doesn't."

"When are they moving the body to a funeral home?"

"Today, I imagine."

"Can you delay it?"

"Why should I?" Baxter asked sourly.

"Let's say the poor woman's been murdered. We owe her at least that much."

"We? I don't owe her one damn thing."

"Would a court order delay it?"

"I suppose it could. And now you've taken up enough of my time with your fancy guesswork—"

Masuto put down the phone and turned to Beckman. "I took it for granted that Baxter would do an autopsy on Eve Mackenzie. He won't. He says there's no evidence that a crime has been committed, and therefore no legal reason for an autopsy. That means I have to hit Wainwright for permission to delay the funeral, which will leave him pretty unhappy. But I'll get—"

"He can't authorize an autopsy, Masao."

"I know. But maybe he can order a hold on the body before the lawyers grab it. Meanwhile, you go up to Santa Barbara and find the sister and talk her into ordering the autopsy. All she has to do is write the request on her stationery. You witness it. If you can get her in front of a notary public, even better, but not absolutely necessary. If she'll come back with you—well, that's the best way. Her name is Jo Hardin. Talk her into coming back with you or get authorization, and take off now. Let's move while we can, because sooner or later they'll go all out to stop us."

Wainwright listened unhappily. "If we go to pathology at All Saints and put a hold on the body, it's like sticking our hand into a nest of wasps. Suppose we find out that Eve Mackenzie was murdered. Think about it: Star on trial for husband's murder murdered. And you know what we add to that, Masao? She was murdered on the Malibu sheriff's turf and the crime was investigated by the California Highway Patrol, and neither outfit had the brains to find out what was going on. The murder is solved by the Beverly Hills police. We pin an asshole badge on both outfits. But, Masao, it's not our murder. We just happen to exist in the State of California. We got to live with the highway patrol and we got to live with the sheriff, but show them to be assholes—well, as I said, we got to live with them."

"And with ourselves."

"All right, all right." Wainwright sighed and spread his arms. "All the way. She lived here, and we got a right not to have our citizens murdered."

"I'm sorry," Masuto said.

"The hell with sorry. We'll do it the hard way. In this case, everything's going to be the hard way."

"I'm going to see Sweeney. If you can order that hold on the body, I'll pick up the papers and take them to Judge Simpkins myself, and maybe get him to back us up."

Sweeney, the fingerprint man, was skinny, dyspeptic, and slightly paranoid about the fact that Masuto put little stock in fingerprints at the scene of a crime. He was defensive the moment Masuto set foot in the small room he called his laboratory, and he stood silent and suspicious, glaring at Masuto.

"Just a small favor, Officer Sweeney," Masuto said in his most beguiling tone. "I'd like to have the Robert Mackenzie fingerprint file."

"The what?"

"The fingerprints of the dead man, Robert Mackenzie."

"You mean the one whose wife scragged him?"

"If you put it that way, yes."

"There ain't no file."

"You mean no background information, but you do have the prints?" Masuto said, clinging to hope.

"No."

"No what?"

"No prints," Sweeney said.

"You're telling me that you have no prints of Robert Mackenzie?"

"That's what I'm telling you, Sergeant."

"All right," Masuto said coldly. "Suppose you tell me how it happened."

"In the first place, Sergeant, before you jump all over me, you got to remember that it is not procedure to take the prints of murder victims. Sometimes we do it, sometimes we don't."

"Didn't Detective Beckman tell you that he wanted to match Mackenzie's prints with a set of prints from the Fenwick Works?"

"Yes."

"And didn't he tell you to pick up the dead man's prints?"

"Yes."

"Then where the devil are they?"

"Now, just wait a minute, Sergeant. I follow procedure. When Detective Beckman told me that he couldn't get the prints from Fenwick, I destroyed the prints I took from the dead man. We got no procedure for filing prints for murder victims. We don't even have a file for it."

Of all problems that were a part of his work, Masuto was least equipped to deal with stupidity. He had always tried not to hate Sweeney. He tried not to hate him now. He tried to understand him, to sympathize with him, to approach the matter as a sincere Zen Buddhist should. It simply did not work, and after a long moment and several deep breaths, he said quietly, "Sweeney, have you ever taken the prints of a man dead two months?"

"What?"

"Didn't you hear me, Officer Sweeney? Robert Mackenzie has been dead two months."

"Then how in hell can I take his fingerprints?"

"That is up to you, isn't it? I intend to exhume the body this afternoon, and I expect you to be there with your trusty fingerprint kit."

"Dead two months, he won't have no fingers!" Sweeney shouted.

"We'll just have to wait and see, won't we?" Masuto looked at his watch. "I think about four o'clock this afternoon. I want you to be ready with your equipment."

"He'll be rotten, Masuto, rotten! He will stink!"

"We'll manage."

Back in Wainwright's office, Masuto presented his case for exhumation.

"You have to?" Wainwright asked moodily.

"I must have the prints. Captain, this whole crazy puzzle rests on a question of identity. I'm convinced the dead man isn't Mackenzie. Then who is he? When we know that, I think we'll know who killed him and why."

"All right, I can give you a police order for the exhumation, but since the case is still in the court, at least technically, even with Eve Mackenzie dead, you have to get Geffner to countersign it. That puts us on safer ground, and the way this case is moving, I'm not giving up any safe ground unless I have to."

At that moment a uniformed patrolman, Oscar Clint by name, put his head into Wainwright's office and said, "Oh, there you are, Sergeant. Your car is blocking mine."

"I'll move it—"

"Give him the key," Wainwright said, "and let's finish with these requests. I got to fill the city manager in on this, so let's get both these orders out of the way before I'm canned."

Masuto tossed the car keys to Clint, who caught them and closed the door.

"You sign right here," Wainwright said to him. "You're the officer in charge. This one for holding the body goes to Judge Simpkins for his signature. The other one, as I said, gets Geffner's signature. Masao, I'm pushing you on this one because I feel we're in some kind of a race. We stop and they—"

He never finished. The explosion rocked the whole building. Masuto raced outside, Wainwright after him, down a staircase packed with police, office help, frightened people.

Outside, where the cars were parked, lay the twisted, blasted remains of Masuto's Datsun. The first flames were licking at the wreck as Masuto, Wainwright, and two other officers fought to get the door open. Then someone passed Masuto a crowbar, which he drove into the door and literally tore it from its frame. They pulled Oscar Clint out of the wreckage, gently, carefully, but it was too late. He was already dead.

11

There were things to do. An ambulance had to be summoned to take away the broken remains of what had been Oscar Clint, and Wainwright had to rehearse what he would say to Mrs. Clint, who was the mother of four children. Statements had to be given, newspaper and television people satisfied, and Mr. Abramson, the city manager, spoken to with whatever explanations could be mustered. There had been some minor cuts from flying glass, and around the city hall, of which the police station was part, several cases of hysteria. As one of the newspaper people wrote, "Generally speaking, Beverly Hills is the most peaceful place in the world. This day was an exception."

But when Wainwright asked Abramson, "Do you want me to pull everyone off it and let it sit? That's what they want. That's why they tried to kill Masuto." The city manager shook his head.

"No, sir. If they—whoever they are—can come in here and turn the place into a slaughterhouse, it won't be worth very much to live here. Let's just say we're protecting the price of the property, because I hate classy sentiments."

Masuto, in the room by virtue of being the target, said, "They'll try again."

"You could take another month off," Wainwright said.

"I had my vacation."

"Bring him or them in," Abramson said. "I'll back you up to the hilt. We'll all sleep better when it's done."

With one thing and another it was almost noontime before Masuto left the station house and drove out to his home in Culver City. His two children were at lunch when he got there. Kati opened the door for him, and he asked angrily, "Is that how you open a door? Someone rings the bell, and you don't ask who it is—you just open the door?"

"Masao, why are you shouting at me? We live on a quiet street in Culver City, not in some jungle."

"No, we live in a jungle," he said, pushing by her into the house. "Close the door and listen to me. As soon as the children finish eating, pack a bag for each of them and pack a bag for yourself. I'm taking the three of you to Uncle Toda's place."

Uncle Toda, Masao's mother's brother, owned an orange grove at the northern end of the San Fernando Valley. He was very fond of Kati and her children, even though, as an old man who had lived through the difficult years of World War II, and had spent two of those years in an internment camp, he looked dubiously upon his nephew's role as a policeman. Nevertheless there were areas in which he admired Masuto, and when his nephew telephoned him about the possibility of Kati and the two children visiting for a few days, he and his wife received the suggestion with pleasure.

But now Kati asked, "How? Have I ceased to exist as a person? You don't ask me—you don't tell me why you have made this decision. Well, I can't go. There are only five days before the children must return to school. There is the party at the center downtown, and the Japanese festival in Anaheim, and I promised them—"

"Stop it!" Masuto interrupted. "I have no time to argue."

Kati stared at him in astonishment and not without a little fear. He had never taken such tones with her before, not Masao; other husbands perhaps, but not Masao.

"You will have them ready in ten minutes, no longer!" Masuto snapped. "Look upon me as an old-fashioned Japanese husband if you must, and obey me. Do you understand?"

"No," Kati whispered. She was not very frightened, not of her husband nor of other things, but she was a Japanese woman, for all that she had been born in America, and she did what he told her to do. She packed the suitcases, scrubbed the children's faces, closed the windows in the little cottage, and followed her husband through the door.

Outside, Kati and the children stared at the car that the department had provided as a replacement for Masuto's Datsun.

"Where is your car?" Kati asked.

"We'll talk about it later."

They were in the car, driving toward the freeway, before Kati said softly, "Something very awful?"

"Yes."

The children were silent. They sensed something menacing, but they knew that their father disliked speaking in their presence about his work as a policeman.

"I'm sorry," Masuto said finally. "I behaved badly, but I was worried, and time is of the essence." He spoke very softly, but still the children heard him.

Kati began to cry. The children had never seen their mother cry before. It frightened them.

"Please, don't cry," Masuto said.

"You never spoke to me like that before."

"I never faced anything like this before. But you know I love you, Kati. You and the children are precious to me."

"Where is your car?"

"We'll go to Uncle Toda's place. Then I can tell you what happened."

Gradually, as they drove north, the children's glumness disappeared. It was far from punishment to spend a week with their Uncle Toda, who had ten acres of orange groves, a holding pond where they could swim, a wife who adored them and spoiled them, and an endless fund of stories about the old days; and by the time they got there, Uraga and Ana had almost forgotten their mother's unhappiness at this unexpected vacation.

Taking his wife and his uncle aside, away from the charming white cottage and into the edge of the grove, Masuto summed up the events of the past twenty-four hours.

"I think you must know about the danger," he said. "If the danger is too great, I can take Kati and the children somewhere else. I was impetuous in exposing you to the danger. I had no right to do that."

"You had every right, and I am too old to worry about danger," Toda told him.

"We are safe, and they will kill you," Kati said bleakly.

"They will not kill us. Rest assured."

"How can I?"

He took her in his arms and held her very tight. "You are my dear wife. I was almost insane before with the thought that they might get to you first. Now you are safe, and I promise you that I will put an end to this thing."

But driving back to Los Angeles, Masuto wondered whether the odds were not greater on their putting an end to him. For the most part, he accepted the world as it was, with all its horrors and obscenities. That was a policeman's world. Either one accepted that or one did not become a policeman, yet there were times when he could not help longing for a limit to reality. Such longings were not very Zen-like, but neither, he felt, was he a very good Zen Buddhist. He could remember as a small child spending lazy summer weeks at his Uncle Toda's grove. The San Fernando Valley was like a Garden of Eden then—pecan groves, orange groves, peach orchards, the wind full of perfume, the sky blue and clear. Today Uncle Toda's place was one of the last large groves in the Valley. Half a million tract houses covered the Valley like an ugly carpet; the sky was yellow with smog; and "Valley girl" had become a national symbol for insularity and ignorance.

It was after three before Masuto reached Judge Simpkins's chambers in Santa Monica, and fortunately Geffner was with the judge.

"Tying up the loose ends," Geffner explained. "I heard about what happened in Beverly Hills this morning. They don't give up, do they? They weren't warning us. They're dead serious."

"I took a dim view of Geffner's accusations concerning what happened to both of you last night," the judge said. "In light of this morning's events—well—well, for the love of God, Sergeant, who do you think is behind all this?"

"I don't know."

"Fenwick? They're a company. Yes, they do Pentagon work, but so do a thousand other companies."

"I was thinking about that," Masuto said. "There were two black limousines and two large, hard-looking men employed as drivers. We leaped to the conclusion that they had cut our brake lines—deciding that they looked like men who would do a thing like that. It was late and we were tired and frightened and had just almost died. That's what our judgment was worth. When Beckman gets back from Santa Barbara, and if we're lucky, the sister will permit an autopsy. Maybe we'll know something then."

"We're going to clear Eve Mackenzie," Geffner said. "There was no case against her, and speaking for myself, my face is red as hell. I suppose it's no comfort to Eve Mackenzie, but if anyone does care, it was an innocent person who died last night."

Masuto said nothing to that, and a few minutes later, both documents countersigned, he left. The whole business of rehabilitating the dead woman left him cold and not a little disgusted, and it was only after he was well on his way toward All Saints Hospital that he remembered the precautions he had not taken. He had not looked under his car or under the hood for another bomb, and why should he imagine that they did not know about his substitute car—a Ford—and his itinerary. He shook his head unhappily, provoked with himself, with his inability to accept the danger he was in, once he felt satisfied that his wife and children were safe.

He had often said that where professional killers were engaged there was actually no way to protect their potential victim. His only security, he felt, was in moving quickly, very quickly, and unraveling the knot of this very strange case. But why himself as a target? Actually, his first real involvement in the case had been when he met Geffner the previous day, and why should they try to kill him rather than Geffner? What did Geffner know? Whatever it was, Geffner had not told him. They might well imagine that Geffner had told him, and of course it had to be their belief that Geffner had talked. It could be nothing else.

His speed slowed. Driving east on Wilshire Boulevard, he had just about reached the veterans cemetery, where thousands of crosses bore witness to the virtue of war. He pulled over to the curb and sat for a long moment with his chin on his clenched fist. Then he turned the Ford around and drove back to Santa Monica. Judge Simpkins was surprised to see him.

"Mr. Geffner?" Masuto asked him.

"Gone. Left here right after you."

"Do you know where he went, Your Honor?"

"I'm afraid not."

"Do you know where his home is?"

"Why don't you talk to my secretary, Sergeant. She has that kind of information."

Outside in the anteroom, the secretary, a bright-eyed Chicano lady of about thirty, said pleasantly, "You're a Nisei, aren't you, Sergeant. And me a Chicano—almost makes you feel we're going somewhere. Why do you want to know about Mark Geffner? Going to arrest him?"

"I want to keep him alive."

"Somebody want to waste him?"

"Possibly."

"Why? He's a sweetheart. Why should anyone want to kill him? I will tell you something, Sergeant Masuto, the whole world has gone bonkers. I'll tell you something else. Nobody needs a reason to kill anyone. They just do it. How about this lunatic who took his rifle up over Sepulveda and spent a whole hour shooting motorists until the cops got him. He killed five people."

"About Mr. Geffner, where does he live?"

"He lives in Mandeville Canyon, but he's not there now. He's on his way to Santa Barbara."

"Do you know why?"

"I think he's got a lady there. But, look, Sergeant, you're not getting anything from me, and if you really have to find Mr. Geffner before someone gets to him, you should talk to his secretary. She knows a lot more about him than I do."

"He's not married, is he?"

"No. Let me try his office. His secretary's name is Lucy Sussman." She dialed the number, and then told Lucy Sussman, "Honey, this is Rosita, over at Judge Simpkins's office. I got a Sergeant Masuto from the Beverly Hills cops who thinks your boss is in trouble." She paused and listened. "No, not that kind of trouble. Yeah—" She turned to Masuto. "You were with Mr. Geffner last night?"

Masuto nodded.

"Same guy, yes." She handed the telephone to Masuto.

"Sergeant," Lucy Sussman said, "I don't know what to tell you. He's very disturbed. He's frightened, too, so I can believe it when Rosita says he's in danger. He's in Santa Barbara, but I have no address or phone number for him there."

"Does he go there often?"

"No, only the past two months—maybe less, maybe six, seven weeks."

"Would that coincide with his involvement with the Mackenzie case?"

There was a long pause, and then the voice on the telephone said, "I don't know that I should be giving you any information of this kind, and certainly I can't give you confidential information of any kind."

"I'm not asking for confidential information. I simply want to reach Mr. Geffner."

"I can't help you. I don't know where he is."

12

Masuto gave up hunting for Geffner and drove to All Saints Hospital. This time he looked under his car and under the hood, shrugging off the fact that from here on his behavior would be slightly paranoid. He was not the only one with a trace of paranoia. When he handed the court order to Dr. Baxter, the medical examiner snorted bitterly.

"You sweethearts spend your days thinking up ways to make my life impossible. In one hour from now the hearse from the Bethlehem Funeral Chapel will be here for her body. You have an order; they have an order. Just tell me, my brilliant Oriental swami, what do I do?"

"This order is countersigned by Judge Simpkins."

"Their order will come from the sheriff's office. They covered the accident. They sent the body here; they release it."

"Our order takes precedence."

"And for how long am I supposed to fight for possession of the body?"

Masuto looked at his watch. "It's four-twenty now. Beckman should be back from Santa Barbara no later than five. Well, let's say that by five-thirty I should be able to tell you to go ahead with the autopsy or release the body."

"That will make me reasonably happy."

"Did you examine Mrs. Mackenzie's body at all, Doctor?"

"I'm a pathologist, not a ghoul. If I'm instructed to do an autopsy, I do an autopsy. If I am not instructed to do one, I leave the body alone."

"Yes, of course," Masuto said. He had years of practice dealing with Dr. Baxter. Baxter was a part-time medical examiner who bitterly resented the fact that Beverly Hills, which he regarded as a somewhat wealthier place than Saudi Arabia, refused to employ him on a full-time basis, claiming that there were simply too few murders to justify it. But Baxter was very good—good enough for his fits of anger and contempt to be tolerated.

"But," Masuto went on apologetically, "even without an autopsy I know how much you can deduce from a cadaver. You know, her car was not badly smashed at all. It was one of those lovely little two-seat Mercedes. The windshield was smashed, but not the car's frame."

"Really?" Baxter's interest was awakened. "Did the car fall through the air?"

"No. Oh, no. It rolled down a steep angle and crashed into a stand of mesquite."

Baxter thought for a while before saying, "She was out, if that's what you're looking for, Masuto. If she had been wearing a seat belt or hanging on to the wheel, her injuries would have been different."

"Thanks. And just in the possibility that we may not be able to do an autopsy, how could she start to drive away and then pass out?"

"There are twenty answers to that question. She might have had a heart attack; she might have had a few drinks and some Nembutal on top of it. They might have slipped her something with an enteric coating, and just in case you don't know what an enteric coating is, I'll explain. It's a coating for a pill that dissolves at a certain speed, depending on how thick you make it. You can take some deadly poison that kills instantly, wrap it up in enteric coating, give it to someone, and have it kill them five minutes or an hour later. But maybe one day you'll develop some minimal intelligence in your own outfit, and I won't have to solve every problem you come up with."

"Yes, possibly," Masuto agreed. "Just one more thing, Doctor. You refer to what they gave her. You conclude it's murder?"

"I don't even have to be smart for that."

"Smarter than the sheriff's deputies."

"There you're dealing with real class."

A TV sound truck was still parked outside the police station when Masuto returned, and a man with a microphone cornered him. He had been waiting for hours and he would not be put off.

"You are Detective Sergeant Masuto?"

"I have no comment," Masuto said. "There's a public relations officer inside."

"Were they trying to kill you instead of Officer Clint? Was it the wrong car and the right man? Come on, Officer, give me a break. I've been waiting five hours for you to return."

Masuto pushed past him and went inside. Wainwright cornered him in the hall. "Abramson's burning mad about Clint being killed. He said we either bring the killer in or there'll be hell to pay with the whole department, and at this point he doesn't give one goddamn about what the State Department or the White House has to say. He went with me to see Clint's wife, and there's something I don't want to go through again. So be careful, Masao, be damn careful. And by the way, what did you say to Sweeney?"

"Can you imagine that he didn't have Mackenzie's prints?"

"We went over that. What did you say to him?"

"I told him he'd have to take the prints now."

"Oh, I see. It didn't occur to me that Mackenzie's been in the ground two months. What in hell happens to a body in two months, Masao?"

"Your guess is as good as mine. But we'll see."

"Sweeney's sick. He's been throwing up. He never had a strong stomach, and I guess thinking about the corpse got to him. I sent him home."

"Captain, I must have those prints."

"You got the exhumation order?"

"Right here in my pocket."

"Okay. Young Anderson spent a year with the paramedics before he became a cop, and he's been helping Sweeney and he's not afraid of cadavers. He'll go with you. Beckman telephoned out to Forest Lawn and they'll have gravediggers waiting for you. But try to do it quick."

"Where's Beckman?"

"Inside. I'll tell Anderson to meet you downstairs, and if you see someone crawling around your car, it's a mechanic from the city motor pool. Abramson is determined no more cars will blow up in our faces."

Beckman was on the phone to his wife, explaining. It sometimes appeared to Masuto that the best part of Sy Beckman's life was spent on the telephone, explaining to his wife his whereabouts for the past twenty-four hours.

"No," Beckman said patiently, "there is just no way I can get home in time to be a fourth for bridge. Where am I going? I'll tell you where I'm going. I'm going to dig up a cadaver." He was not believed, and his explanations continued. Finally out of it, he said to Masuto, "Next time around, a Japanese girl. You don't get that from Kati."

Masuto had heard it before. "Tell me about Santa Barbara."

"Well, she doesn't actually live in Santa Barbara. She lives in Montecito. That's a community or neighborhood or whatever just on this side of Santa Barbara. Beautiful spot. You ever been there?"

Masuto nodded.

"You could be a thousand miles from anywhere. A dirt road, and then a house of cut stone, with a million roses, a tiled roof, a terrace of Mexican tiles—and this Jo Hardin. You say to yourself, Eve Mackenzie was a beauty, the sister must be a plain Jane. No, sir. Just as pretty as her sister. Supposed to be fifty-one. You'd never believe it. She could pass for thirty. Ever heard of a famous Western badman and outlaw, name of John Wesley Hardin? She claims to be a relative of his."

"Did she agree to the autopsy?" Masuto demanded impatiently.

"No luck there. She claims there is no reason for it, that her sister suffered enough. I talked and argued, but she wouldn't give an inch."

"But why? She knows her sister died a violent death. She might well have surmised that her sister was framed. Why shouldn't she agree to an autopsy?"

"I tried, Masao."

"Did you make it plain to her that we're convinced that her sister was murdered?"

"I did. She just kept saying that she wanted to forget the whole thing."

"What was her attitude? Did she appear to have an affection for her sister?"

"Not much. She's a pretty cold fish."

"Does she live alone there?"

"As far as I could tell. Well, not absolutely alone."

"What does that mean?"

"Well, like I said, Masao, there's a dirt road leads up to the place. Pretty narrow, so if you're going to pass another car, you got to slow it down almost to a walk. Well, I was leaving there when I saw a car coming, and I had to slow it down, like I said, almost to a walk. So I had a good look at who was in the car. You want to take a guess?"

"Mark Geffner."

Beckman's face fell. "How did you know?" he whispered.

"Did he see you?"

"Had to. What made you say Geffner?"

"A guess. And knowing you, Sy, you've gone into his background. What have you got?"

"Just what popped up on the computer. He's Mr. Clean. U.C.L.A., Stanford Law, Judge Advocate in Vietnam, and then the state. He's forty-six years old, divorced four years ago, and that's it."

"No, only the beginning," Masuto said.

13

Masuto, Beckman, and Anderson waited while the city mechanic went over their cars with a fine-tooth comb. Then Masuto decided that they would all go in Beckman's car. "You drive. I want to think," Masuto told Beckman.

"I like to think while I'm driving," Beckman said.

"Yes, that's one way. Another way is to empty your mind, stop your thoughts."

"Then how're you thinking, if you'll forgive me, Sergeant?" Anderson asked.

"Well, you are, but in another way. You're letting something happen in your mind. In a way, it's what most people do. You try to remember something and it's impossible. Then you put it away, and then suddenly you have the answer, apparently out of nowhere. But your mind does it for you. Maybe it will do it for me. There must be some sanity, some logic, to this wretched business."

"Why? We live in a world full of lunatics."

Masuto shrugged, closed his eyes, and sank back in his seat while Beckman drove over Coldwater Canyon into the Valley below, where the smog lay like a heavy yellow blanket. Masuto finally opened his eyes as they left the Ventura Freeway and turned north on Barham.

"Got it?" Beckman asked him.

"Not a glimmer."

"You think we can get this done before dark, Masao?"

"We'll try. It shouldn't take more than half an hour or so."

"Are you nervous, kid?" Beckman asked Anderson.

"A little. I never did anything like this before. I asked to work with

Officer Sweeney because I heard he's due to retire next year, but until now I've only taken prints off people who are alive."

"Nothing to it. They don't pull away when they're dead."

"But this one's been dead a long time. You think he's got a record, Sergeant?" he asked Masuto.

Masuto smiled and shook his head. "I don't know what to think. We'll see."

It seemed there was always smog at the eastern side of the San Fernando Valley. Masuto could remember a time when there had been no smog in the Valley—but then so many other things had changed.

They turned into Forest Lawn Drive, and a few minutes later they were entering the cemetery, halted by a guard and then waved on to a chorus of alto voices singing an obviously specifically composed song about a host of angels welcoming the loved ones into the heavenly gates.

"Loudspeakers concealed in the ground," Beckman explained.

At the cemetery office, which was built in a strange, Romanesque style, the cemetery director was waiting for them. He was appropriately a tall, thin, somber-looking man, and beside him, a man in black with a ministerial collar stood with his hands folded.

"I'm Detective Sergeant Masuto. This is Detective Beckman and Officer Anderson, who will take the fingerprints. Since it's almost seven o'clock, I think we should start immediately."

"Yes—yes, indeed. You'll be pleased to know that after your Captain Wainwright telephoned me, I had the gravediggers open the grave."

"Have they removed the coffin?" Masuto demanded, annoyed.

"No, sir—oh, no. No, indeed. But they set up the sacre-lift, our name for the mechanism we use to lower the coffin and the loved one, and that means reeving the canvas straps under the coffin. You can't just lift the coffin out of the grave—not a large bronze coffin that weighs a quarter of a ton."

"Can we get on with it?"

"Certainly, certainly, Detective Masuto. Only one or two small matters. The gravediggers go off at four o'clock. That's union rules—nothing I can do about that. Which means double time, fourteen dollars an hour, and I'm afraid you must sign this acknowledgment and order before I let you go to Mr. Mackenzie's grave." He held out a clipboard. Masuto scanned the paper, then signed it, wondering how Wainwright would respond to ninety dollars for the two gravediggers.

Beckman, standing behind Masuto and looking over his shoulder, answered the question. "He'll take our ass off, Masao."

"We don't get double overtime," Anderson said.

The director now removed the top contract from the clipboard and handed it back to Masuto.

"What's this?"

"The Reverend Peterson here," nodding at the man next to him. "It's cemetery policy that no grave should be opened or closed without an accredited clergyman present. Reverend Peterson's fee is only thirty dollars, little enough when you consider he's been waiting since our normal closing time of four o'clock. And may I remind you that I am taking no fee for my extra hours, but acting out of a devotion to a civilized and law-abiding country."

"For which we are grateful," Masuto said, signing a bill in which the City of Beverly Hills was charged for thirty dollars for the services of Reverend Avril Peterson. "Now, if you would please lead us to the Mackenzie grave, we can get this over with."

The director led the way, explaining that ordinarily, even with the judicial order, the close relatives would have to be notified. "We do not play dirty pool with the dearly beloved," he said, choosing, Masuto decided, a very odd metaphor indeed. "But do you know, Sergeant, Mr. Mackenzie had no relatives—close or otherwise, that is—after the death of his wife. What a pity that a man should live that way. Don't you think so, Reverend Peterson?"

"Oh, yes. The family is the rock of hope," Reverend Peterson said.

"All alone. No one. Do you know, I called the Fenwick Works. Lovely people. Such lovely, cooperative people. They put me through to the manager himself. There was no need for that. I simply asked for the personnel department, and they put me through to Mr. Soames." He turned to Masuto, who had stopped short.

"You called Fenwick and spoke to Mr. Soames?" Masuto said icily.

"Oh, yes—yes, indeed."

"And you told him why you were calling? That the Beverly Hills police were going to exhume the body?"

"Oh, yes. I didn't think it was a secret."

"And when did you do this?"

"After your Captain Wainwright called me. An hour ago?"

"It would take them almost an hour to drive here," Beckman said.

"You spoke to Soames?" Masuto reminded him. "What exactly did you say to him?"

"What I said, of course."

"Would you please repeat what you said as exactly as you can." They were in sight of the grave now, a metal frame around it, a pile of fresh-dug dirt alongside and two gravediggers waiting. From some hidden loudspeaker, a baritone voice, muted, told anyone listening that "seated one day at the organ, I was weary and ill at ease, and my fingers wandered idly over the noisy keys."

"I don't see what that has to do with anything," the director protested.

"Let's say out of your devotion to civilization, as you put it before. And isn't there any way to turn off that damned voice?"

"It will stop automatically, Sergeant Masuto, and I am not surprised that an Oriental does not respond to so intrinsically Western a thing as *The Lost Chord.*"

"Of course. We all have limitations. To get back to Mr. Soames."

"If you wish. I told him that I was attempting to locate some relative of Mr. Robert Mackenzie. He asked why—oh, very politely—and I told him that Captain Wainwright of the Beverly Hills police had called me and informed me that Sergeant Masuto would be coming out to exhume the body and take fingerprints and that I might have the grave opened, since it was late in the day."

"And what did he say to that?"

"Mr. Soames?"

"Yes, Mr. Soames."

"Oh, he said that as far as he knew, Mr. Mackenzie had no relatives other than his wife—no blood relatives at all."

"And that's all?"

"Well, he did say that he was sorry I was being put to so much trouble."

"Thoughtful of him," Beckman said.

Now a great orange globe of a sun was sinking toward the hills that made the western wall of the San Fernando Valley, and Masuto said to Beckman, "Sy, get the coffin up and opened and get the prints and let's get out of here before dark." He didn't add that Forest Lawn turned his stomach and offended every decent sensibility.

"Did Mr. Soames appear in any way disturbed?" he asked the cemetery director.

"I hardly think so."

Which, again, made Masuto wonder as he stared at the emerging coffin. They all moved closer to the grave and stood in silence as the coffin rose smoothly, cranked up by a pair of winches, hand operated by the two gravediggers. Finally the coffin hung on a level with the ground, and the gravediggers slid it off the mechanism.

"I hope your Officer Anderson has a strong stomach. These things can be upsetting."

"Open it," Masuto said to the gravediggers.

It was a large, ornate bronze coffin. It had four bolts on each side, and when they were removed and the heavy cover lifted, the men standing around were braced for horror and disgust. But aside from a profusion of quilted white silk and velvet, the coffin was empty.

14

Wainwright was so intrigued by the empty coffin that he forgot to complain about overtime for the gravediggers. Abramson, the city manager, had been in to see Wainwright about illegal parking around some of the larger hotels, and when he heard about Masuto's expedition, he decided to await his return. Like Wainwright, the notion of the big bronze coffin being empty fascinated him.

"Who ordered the burial and paid for it?" Wainwright asked.

Masuto shook his head. He had been in Japan. Beckman said, "That was Eve Mackenzie."

"But why that coffin? You say it weighed a quarter of a ton."

"Because it would still carry heavy, even without the body."

"What does one of those things cost?"

"Plenty," Abramson said. "I just buried my mother-in-law. She was a religious lady and specified a plain wooden box, but I priced a few of the fancy ones. You could be buried in a Cadillac for that kind of money."

"Do you suppose we'll ever turn up the body, Masao?"

"No. They don't want the body or the prints found. They probably wrapped it in chains, took it out in a boat, and gave it to the sharks. No, we'll never see it."

"Why?" Abramson demanded. "You keep saying *they*, Sergeant. Who are they?"

"I don't know. I know what they do, and I'm beginning to understand how they think, but who they are—"

"And now, with the body gone, the murderer goes free?"

"No, not quite, Mr. Abramson. What they say about the absence of a corpse doesn't apply here. We know the murder was committed. It doesn't matter whether the body is buried at Forest Lawn or at the bottom of the Pacific."

"Then we can find the killer and convict him?"

"No, I don't think so."

"Masao," Wainwright exploded, "is this another one of your damn tricks? Do you know who killed Mackenzie?"

"Even if I know, it doesn't help. We have no evidence, and before we're able to scrape some up, the killer will be dead."

There was a long moment of silence while they all stared at Masuto, and then Wainwright said coldly, "What in hell are you talking about?"

Masuto was tired, close to exhaustion after a day that had been too long and too terrifying, and in no mood to argue or convince. "All things," he said without enthusiasm, "have a pattern and a rhythm. We live in patterns and think in patterns and act in patterns. They have a pattern. Their minds are lazy but brutal. They kill for solutions. They act hastily. The charade in the bathtub was clumsy and hasty. They felt that the man in the tub was dangerous, so they killed him. Now they will kill the killer, because the killer is dangerous."

"Goddamnit, Masao, if you know who it is, bring him in. We'll cook up a charge."

"We can't do that," Abramson said. "Not in Beverly Hills, Captain Wainwright. You know that."

"It wouldn't matter," Masuto said moodily.

"The hell with it," Wainwright said. "Let's call it a day."

"The mechanic's still there," Abramson told them. "He'll check your cars."

Walking out of the police station with Beckman, Masuto asked him, "About Mackenzie's birthplace—did you say Glasgow?"

"Edinburgh."

"Where did you get that?"

"From Mrs. Scott. Fenwick confirmed it."

"Ah, so! Very interesting. That they gave you, but not the fingerprints. Did you also get the date he arrived in America?"

"Nineteen sixty-one. He was thirty-one."

"Also from Fenwick?"

"Oh, yes. They were cooperative."

The mechanic informed them that both of their cars were clean.

"I'll see you in the morning, Sy," Masuto said.

"By the way, I almost forgot. Polly said Doc Baxter would like to see you. He'll be working late. This late—well, I don't know."

It was enough to prompt Masuto to drive to All Saints Hospital. In any case, he had no place to go. His home was empty; his wife and children were with Uncle Toda in San Fernando. It was a new situation for him. He was very much a householder, and his little cottage in Culver City was his rock. Now, suddenly, he was alone, homeless, for he had no desire to go home and sleep in an empty house—a place at this moment not only empty but very dangerous.

At the pathology room in the basement of All Saints a lonely figure sat at a laboratory table under a bright light, peering into a microscope. In all the years he had worked with Dr. Baxter, Masuto had never inquired as to whether the small, bitter medical examiner had a wife or a family. That was poor human behavior on his own part, he told himself, and even worse Zen behavior—at which point in Masuto's thinking, the doctor looked up and said, "It took you long enough to get here, my Oriental Sherlock. Did you expect me to wait all night?"

"You mean you were actually waiting for me?"

"I wasn't sitting here whistling Dixie. Now, listen to me. I was letting you and your boss, the brilliant Wainwright, who is possibly brain-damaged according to his behavior, run around in circles, and then my conscience took over and I reminded myself that we're on the same side. The point is, Masuto, you don't need an autopsy for what you want. I simply took some blood from Mrs. Mackenzie and I ran a lot of tests. She was not poisoned or drugged, unless you think of alcohol as both of those things, which it is. Eve Mackenzie was drunk—sodden, stinking drunk. She was absolutely loaded—with nothing but alcohol. Now, if you're going to ask me whether she could drive a car in her condition—well, I would have to know what kind of a drunk she was."

"You just told me that," Masuto protested.

"No, sir. I told you how much alcohol there was in her blood. What kind of a drunk she was is something else. There are folks who have that kind of alcohol level in their blood, and they would get up out of a chair and fall flat on their face. Someone else walks away and you don't even know he's loaded. Tell me, did her sister approve the autopsy?"

"No."

"Now you know why."

"You mean her sister knew she was an alcoholic, and she figured now that Eve is dead there's no need for the world to know."

"That would be my guess."

"And you think she could get in her car, start the motor, drive two or three miles, and then pass out?"

"Absolutely."

"And you feel nothing more could be gained by an autopsy?"

Baxter shrugged. "What more do you want? Conceivable but not likely. I don't think she had any drugs. The liquor did it."

Masuto thanked him. "I'm very grateful."

"Tell that to Abramson. Remind him that what I'm paid by the richest city in America is a national disgrace."

15

Back in his car, Masuto sat and brooded. He reminded himself of an ancient Zen story. The student comes to the Zen master and says to him, "Master, my father sends me here to study Zen, but why should I study Zen?" To which the Roshi replies, "So that when the times comes, you will not be afraid to die."

Masuto did not know whether or not he was afraid to die. The times when he faced death left no moments for reflection, and he had always considered himself a very poor Zen Buddhist; but he was also a practical person, and he felt that to go home to his house in Culver City tonight would be foolhardy indeed. Instead, he drove downtown, taking precautions to see that he was not followed.

It was almost eleven o'clock when he reached the Zendo in downtown Los Angeles. The door to the meditation hall was always open, and he went in there, taking off his shoes first. The meditation hall was thirty feet long and twelve feet wide. Running the length of the room on either side, there was a section five feet wide and raised six inches from the ground. A single lamp lit the polished wood of the hall with a soft, flickering radiance.

Masuto took a pillow and mat from where they were piled at the end of the hall, set the small round pillow on the mat, took off his jacket, loosened his belt, and then settled himself into the lotus position. He began his meditation, and then found himself falling asleep. The soft light in the long empty hall had a hypnotic effect, and it had been an endless day since the bomb planted in his car blew Officer Clint into eternity. He fought to stay awake. Another Zen tale told of the monk who, having slept through his meditation, cut his eyelids off in remorse.

A story Masuto hated, but which came to his mind now as he fought to remain awake—even resorting to the device of counting each breath.

It did not help, and a voice speaking in Japanese reached into his consciousness, saying, "Masao, Masao, what must I think to see a man pretending to meditate and sound asleep, with a gun under his arm in this place where no weapon is permitted?"

It was always difficult for Masuto to understand Japanese, and coming out of sleep even more difficult; and now he could only mumble, "Roshi, I slept in my meditation."

"It is past midnight," the old man who was the Roshi there told him. "Go home and sleep, Masao."

"I sent my wife and children away. My home is a dangerous place."

The old man shook his head unhappily. "Why must you earn a living this way, Masao?"

"It is my karma."

"Don't talk nonsense to me!" he snapped. "It is your choice. Now, come to my house and I'll spread a mat on the floor for you. Sleep is not meditation, and I think you need sleep more."

Masuto slept well on the floor of the little house behind the Zendo hall, and in the morning, after a bowl of rice and several cups of tea, he looked upon the world more cheerfully. He put through a call to Kati, who informed him that Uraga and Ana were already swimming in the holding pond and very happy, and Uncle Toda and his wife were darling to them, but that she, Kati, wanted to be home with her husband where she properly belonged.

"Another few days," Masuto promised her.

"And you will be careful. Every time I think of the work you do, I die a little."

"I am the most careful man in California."

Since he was already in downtown Los Angeles, he stopped off at Fred Toyota's place for a shave. Toyota was a cousin of Kati's three or four times removed, somewhere in the tangle of relationships that Japanese families clung to, a plump, birdlike little man, who guessed that it was the Zendo that had brought Masuto down here "where a haircut is still five dollars—and just as good as the thirty-dollar cuts in Beverly Hills. But myself, Masao, I'm a Presbyterian. I have given up that old-country nonsense—"

"Very commendable. I'm in a hurry."

"When I shave, I talk."

Humbled but clean-shaven, Masuto drove to the police station in Beverly Hills. Beckman was sitting in his office, feet up on his desk, reading the sports section of the *Los Angeles Times,* and he greeted Masuto with the proposition that one can't say never. "I mean, Masao, that if anyone had told me that football players would form a union and strike, I would have said never. Absolutely never."

"You're right," Masuto said. "You can't say never. Now, tell me something. What's the situation at the Mackenzie house? From the time of his murder."

"You know," Beckman said, dropping his feet and putting the newspaper aside, "I never thought of that. It is goddamn strange."

"What is?"

"Well, look—you heard the testimony the other day in court. The whole damn thing was Feona Scott's little ploy. Suppose Eve Mackenzie could have been found guilty. It would have been Scott who put her away. But Eve was out on bail, and there they were, both of them living in the Mackenzie house."

"You're sure of that?"

"Yeah—"

"And you never thought it strange before?"

"I suppose I should have. But nothing in this case makes sense."

"Or everything. I'll tell you what I want you to do, Sy. Go out to Santa Monica and see Judge Simpkins and get a search warrant for the Mackenzie house. Then go in there and find something that will give us a break in this case."

"What?"

"I don't know. But there has to be something in that house that will shed a little light on the fact that a man who isn't Robert Mackenzie but who everyone wants to dispose of as Robert Mackenzie is murdered in a crazy Rube Goldberg manner, and everyone—accused, accusers—everyone loves everyone, except that someone wants to kill anyone who puts his nose into it. So, damn it, be careful! We've Clint's funeral tomorrow. I don't want to go to yours the next day."

"Where will you be?"

"I'm going across to the library, and then I'll be back here."

The Beverly Hills library is unique, one of the finest public libraries in California, and housed in a splendid building across the street from the police station. The quality of the library grew out of two things; the wealth of the town, and the patronage of motion picture and television people, who needed a well-equipped library close at hand. At the cost of twenty-five dollars a year, a non-resident could be a member, but Masuto's membership derived from his job. He was an assiduous reader and a familiar figure at the library, especially to Miss Clarissa Jones.

Miss Jones confirmed Masuto's belief that marriages should be arranged. Miss Jones, slender, very attractive behind her glasses, tall, and possessed of a decent sense of humor, was still unmarried at age thirty-seven because, as she put it, she had never gotten around to it. Masuto always thought of it as a tragic waste, and even today the thought crossed his mind as he informed Miss Jones, the librarian he most preferred, that he was interested in Scotland.

"Scotland, Sergeant? That's a large subject. We must have two hundred books on Scotland. Have you ever been there?"

Masuto shook his head. "Not England, not Scotland. I am very insular, Miss Jones."

"I don't believe that for a minute. Suppose we narrow it down. Where in Scotland—or just Scotland?"

"Edinburgh."

"Well, you've just lucked out, Sergeant. I took my vacation last month, and a week of it was in Edinburgh. Shall I inform you, or do you want a book?"

"I haven't time for a book."

Miss Jones whispered a few words to another lady behind the desk, and then led Masuto to a table. "All right, here goes for a quick rundown on Edinburgh. Ask away."

"How large?"

"Half a million people."

"Crime?"

"Not so I noticed, but you might say that in L.A. too, if you were a tourist. Not too much, I'd say."

"Nice people?"

"Delightful, but I'm prejudiced. I'm half Welsh and half Scot."

"Factory town?"

"No, no, indeed. That would be Glasgow. I felt that Edinburgh was one of the loveliest cities I've ever seen. A great old castle sits above the town, and its location on the Firth of Forth is simply splendid."

"And what about hospitals, medical places? Are they up-to-date?"

"Sergeant, you really don't know much about Scotland. It's not a wild, primitive place, and except for festivals they don't wear kilts, and they really are absolutely civilized. Their hospitals are as good as any in Europe, and in many areas of medicine they have led the world. You should know that both the Welsh and the Scots are very smart people."

"I'm delighted to hear that. Then you don't think it would be ridiculous on my part to call the chief of police in Edinburgh and ask about records half a century old?"

"Wow. Is that what you're going to do?"

"I'm thinking about it."

"Not ridiculous at all. But listen carefully, Sergeant. They have a very peculiar accent."

Wainwright, on the other hand, stared at Masuto glumly and asked why he couldn't send a telex.

"I have to talk to him, and then he'll have to call me back."

"To the tune of how much?"

"I don't know—fifty, a hundred, a hundred and fifty—I just can't say."

"We blew a bundle on those damn gravediggers and came up with nothing."

"Not really nothing. We know the grave is empty."

"That'll buy you a stale taco and a flat beer. What pisses me off, Masao, is that I sit here and you stand there and play games about knowing who's running this show—"

"I don't know who's running it. All I can do is make an educated guess about who killed Mackenzie."

"Then educate me, goddamnit!" Wainwright shouted.

"All right. I think that Feona Scott killed him—and it's not Mackenzie. We keep saying Mackenzie. It's another man."

Wainwright pursed his lips and whistled softly. "Feona Scott." He stared with interest at Masuto. "Why Feona Scott?"

"That's it. As I told you, I don't have enough evidence to fill a thimble."

"Then just put it together so that it makes some sense to me, Masao, because the way it is it don't make one damn bit of sense."

"All right. But keep in mind that this is a creation out of the whole cloth. I don't know what happened there at the Mackenzie house that night any more than you do, but I think I see a pattern and I try to fill in on the pattern. Mackenzie, I think, is not home. That's only a guess, because regardless of what Mackenzie is—and I've come to think of him as a cold-blooded bastard—I don't see him moving behind his twin brother and knocking him out with some kind of blunt object. Not that he couldn't kill, but differently. Eve is out of the picture. She was an alcoholic according to Doc Baxter, and that wonderful calm and dignity of hers was probably a habit of desperate concentration to keep from falling over. So that leaves Feona, and I'm quite certain she knocked out the man in the tub."

"And how did she get him into the tub? Granted she's a strong, well-built woman, maybe five foot seven or eight, but Mackenzie weighed over two hundred pounds. I saw the body, Masao. Someone had to undress him and then put him in the tub."

"Not Mackenzie—the twin. We go on with my invention. Mackenzie comes back. The twin is lying there—"

"There was a skull fracture," Wainwright remembered. "He was zapped good and hard."

"Feona has been reading Eve's notebook, which makes more sense as the creation of a drunken mind. She shows the notebook to Mackenzie or he already knows about it. Let's put him into the tub and electrocute him. Follow Eve's formula and Eve has to be charged with the murder."

"Which they must have known would not stand up."

"They needed time," Masuto said. "And they had certain problems. They had to get rid of the twin's body or his clothes. The clothes were easier, and since they couldn't get rid of the body, they left it in the tub and Mackenzie decided to vanish."

"Why? You can't have it that they couldn't get rid of the body, Masao. No, sir. They could have put it in a car and driven somewhere and dumped it."

"Yes."

"Well, damn it, what is it? Yes or no?"

"It could be one of two things. Either they couldn't get rid of the body or they didn't want to. From here on, there's just too much lunacy and uncertainty attached to it. Mackenzie goes to Soames and Fenwick and tells him that he and Feona just murdered his twin brother and framed his wife, Eve, as the killer. Soames understands and approves of this, and he gets all sorts of important people in Washington to jump in and insist that Eve be tried for a crime she could never be convicted of. Eve agrees and accepts the Fenwick lawyer as her defender. The judge decides to throw out the case. Eve has dinner in the Fenwick dining room at Malibu and gets so drunk she drives her car over a cliff and kills herself and when Beckman drives up to Montecito to talk to her sister, who does he see as he is leaving?"

"You tell me."

"Mark Geffner."

"No. No, that's too much."

"Nothing is too much. This whole thing is framed in lunacy."

"And you still feel that Feona Scott will be killed?"

"I'm afraid so," Masuto admitted. "There's a cold-blooded killer at work here. I've been thinking about what you said. What can we do?"

"Truthfully, not much. You know how Abramson feels about false arrest. And suppose we did arrest her. Her lawyer would have her out of jail in an hour. We could put a cop outside the house—"

Masuto shook his head. "That won't help. By the way, who is her lawyer—well, I mean the Mackenzies' lawyer?"

Wainwright furrowed his brow. "If I remember correctly, it was Dave Pringle."

"But Henry Cassell defended her."

"Yes. Pringle's a theatrical lawyer. I suppose if we picked up Feona, Cassell would come around—or maybe not. I don't know. But if we're going to arrest her, we need enough concrete evidence to convince Abramson that we're not just making a grandstand play."

"Yes, I'll try. Meanwhile—"

"Meanwhile, hell. You drop a bombshell about Geffner and then walk out?"

"No, sir. All I know about Geffner is what Beckman told me. He was driving out; Geffner was driving in."

"Did you talk to Geffner?"

"Captain, I returned to Beverly Hills four days ago. Since then, my car has been blown up, someone tried to send me over a cliff in Malibu, I've had to send my wife and children away, I dug up an empty coffin, and I haven't changed my clothes in two days. No, I haven't spoken to Geffner."

"I'm not pushing you, Masao."

"No, I'm pushing because I want to stay alive. What about this call to Scotland?"

"Okay, okay. You got it."

16

But first Masuto looked up Dave Pringle's number and called the lawyer and got through to him without any problem and told him that they were reopening the Mackenzie case.

"I'm glad," Pringle said. "I'm damn glad. And I hope that at the same time you're giving attention to the very strange death of Mrs. Mackenzie. I find the accident that killed her very disturbing. You must know, Detective Masuto, that she was my client, not her husband."

"Yes, I do know that. I have a very strong feeling that a deal of some sort was made with Mrs. Mackenzie, and that she agreed not to fight the indictment in return for—well, I don't know what for. But my feeling is that in return for her silence as to who the man in the tub actually was and in return for her being on trial, it was agreed by Cassell that there would be no contest over her husband's estate. Was Mr. Mackenzie a wealthy man?"

"You appear to know a great deal, Detective Masuto, but before I continue, I would like you to hang up, and I'll call back."

"That's reasonable," Masuto agreed.

Almost five minutes passed before Masuto's phone rang. It was Polly at the switchboard, who said, "Masao, Pringle, the lawyer. He wanted to know everything about you from day one. I'm giving him to you now."

"Sergeant," Pringle said, "how much do you actually know about Eve Mackenzie?"

"I know she was an alcoholic."

"Yes. Well, we tried to keep it a secret and we succeeded pretty well. But she hadn't worked in years, and she had no future in films—poor thing. So many of us loved her, and there was absolutely nothing we could do. There is nothing as awful as giving your heart to an alcoholic. Now, you asked me before whether Mackenzie was a wealthy man. Hardly. He had no money to speak of, although Fenwick paid him a hundred thousand a year. He was a mean, vicious bastard, and if I speak ill of the dead, I do so deliberately. The only kind thing you could say about him is that he left Eve alone and that he did not throw her out. It was his house, and I suspect that there were reasons I don't know for his keeping her there. They never entertained, and the Scott woman was apparently, according to Eve, his mistress. Eve had made a good deal of money in films when she was a star and much in demand, and I did try to husband it, but it was hopeless. She threw it away. The car in which she died used up her last bit of personal funds."

"And the man in the tub?"

"Mackenzie's twin brother. But she told me this under a pledge of silence as her lawyer."

"Then why did she go on trial?"

"Because Soames, the manager at Fenwick, offered her fifty thousand dollars to accept the indictment and keep quiet about the twin brother. He assured her that the case would be thrown out of court, and I agreed with that judgment. Mackenzie also signed a new will, which they backdated, and which leaves the house and a good packet of stock options in Fenwick to Eve. I did not learn about this until after the fact and I was sworn to silence. It was privileged. I would not be telling you this now had it not been for Eve's death the day before yesterday. Poor girl, I wanted desperately for her to have some security, to have the house and a few dollars. Now I feel that this is information the police should have."

"Mr. Pringle," Masuto said slowly, "I'm not trying to be dramatic or to alarm you unnecessarily, but unless you take precautions, an attempt will be made on your life, and very possibly a successful one."

"Come on, Sergeant. I'm a lawyer. I've been involved in legal matters, that's all."

"You have been given very dangerous information. Too dangerous."

"I don't believe that at all. But since you're so sure I'm in danger, what do you think I should do?"

"Yes, I will tell you what to do. The moment we finish, call the *Los Angeles Times*. Give them the whole story, every word, every detail. They'll run it on the front page, and if you live until the paper appears tomorrow, you're safe."

"Sergeant, I can't do that. Look at the position it puts me in. And what does it do to Eve's memory? I would betray her."

"You betrayed her the day you allowed her to go into that stupid charade," Masuto said harshly.

"You can't talk to me like that."

"Why not? You can hang up and brush me off as another arrogant cop. But you're still the target."

"What can I do?"

"Pack a bag, get out to the airport without being followed, and take the next plane to San Francisco. And try to understand what I'm telling you. Eve Mackenzie took you into her confidence, and the information she gave you is dangerous. Now, it's true that I know what you know, and Captain Wainwright knows it too, but the killer isn't aware of that. Go away for a few days."

"I'll think about it."

"You don't believe me, do you?"

"No, Sergeant. I'm afraid not."

"Well, let's say I've done my civic duty."

"If you wish, Sergeant."

Of course, Masuto said to himself. He'd be a fool to believe me. People don't go around killing people senselessly, not in Beverly Hills.

He went into Wainwright's office and asked him whether he knew what time it was in Scotland.

"Haven't you made that call yet?"

"I was talking to Pringle, the lawyer."

"My guess would be somewhere between four and five o'clock in the afternoon. What about Pringle?"

"You know, English is a remarkable language. I don't think there's any word in Japanese that's precisely the equivalent of horse's ass, which you can be and still get through law school."

"What the hell does all that mean?" Wainwright demanded.

"It means that Soames, the manager at Fenwick, offered Eve Mackenzie fifty thousand dollars to keep her mouth shut about the man in the tub being Mackenzie's twin brother and to go on trial until the case was thrown out of court, and this damn fool, Pringle, advised her to accept the offer. And then, when I told him that he knew too much and might be a target, he refused to believe me."

"How about me refusing to believe you?"

"I wouldn't blame you."

"We live in a world of idiots, Masao."

"It's the occupational disease of the human race, but if we could put a uniform in front of his building for the next day or two, it might help keep him alive. His office is in Beverly Hills?"

"Four-fifty North Roxbury. But that means putting a man on overtime."

"Let's be spendthrifts."

"Yeah, what the hell, this case is tearing our budget to shreds, so we might as well go all the way, and I got to have a meeting with Abramson and the city attorney. We never had anything like this before. What the devil was Soames up to with a crazy play like that? And was he breaking the law or not—and who put the body away? I can't make head or tail of this twin-brother business. Can you?"

"I get a glimmer, but then it won't stay with me."

"You know, Masao, I think you got to go out there to Fenwick and put it to Soames just flat out—how about the payment and who in hell cut the brake lines on Geffner's car?"

"I was thinking of that. Of course, they'll deny everything, and with Eve dead—"

"And I want to know what the devil Geffner was doing with her sister."

"That's touchy too. We have no right to question Geffner about anything in Montecito."

"It ties in, doesn't it?"

"Sort of. I suppose I can talk to Geffner."

As he was leaving the room, Wainwright said to Masao, "Tomorrow's poor Clint's funeral. Ten o'clock, Church of Our Lady. He's the first man killed on the force in five years, and it hasn't been nice, Masao. It surely hasn't been nice."

"I have my own guilts."

"Stifle your guilts. You didn't know the car was wired any more than he did."

17

Masuto told the operator that he did not know the man's name, but that Edinburgh, like any other city, must have a chief of police. The operator was not at all sure that there was anyone with that title, and Masuto said he would settle for police headquarters. When a voice with a heavy burr informed him that this was Edinburgh Police, Masuto gave his own title and rank and said that he was calling from police headquarters in Beverly Hills, and since the police station was also by default police headquarters, Masuto was not straying from the fact. After a long, long pause, which Masuto estimated cost the City of Beverly Hills at least five dollars, another voice told him that he was speaking to Inspector Angus Macready.

"Now, are you putting me on?" Macready said to him. "Or am I really speaking to a policeman in Beverly Hills? Because, laddie, if this is your notion of a bloody joke, you will regret it."

"No joke, sir. I am Detective Sergeant Masao Masuto of the Beverly Hills police force."

"Devil take me! What kind of a name is that?"

"Japanese name because my parents were Japanese."

"Would you spell it?"

"Masuto. M-a-s-u-t-o."

"And you're actually a policeman there in Beverly Hills?"

"Yes, absolutely."

"Well, I will be damned! I cannot wait to tell my wife—Beverly Hills."

"Inspector," Masuto began.

"Tell me something. Suppose there I am, walking down the street in Beverly Hills, would I be likely to meet—oh, say, Paul Newman?"

"It could happen, yes. But, Inspector—"

"Robert Redford? Now, there's someone I'd like to meet. Now, suppose my wife and I were to take one of those package trips—"

"Inspector," Masuto said firmly, "I am calling on a most important police matter."

"Of course. Sorry. It's a habit of thinking Americans are very rich."

"We are a small police department with a limited budget, and we are required to account for every long distance call. I would love to chat with you about Beverly Hills, but—"

"Of course. Please, I must apologize. What can I do for you, Sergeant —is it Masuto?"

"Masuto."

"Odd name. Well, here I am at your service."

"Thank you. I have a rather peculiar request, Inspector, but important in a homicide investigation we are conducting. I want to know whether in the year nineteen thirty twins were born to a couple named Mackenzie, or to several couples with that name, and if possible, what has been the history of those twins."

"That's it?"

"Just about."

"Well, that's a tall order, Sergeant. Mackenzie's a common name in Edinburgh, but truthfully I have no notion of how common twins are."

"Can it be done?"

"If our hospitals were computerized, it would be the work of an hour or so. I'm not sure myself what condition the records are in or if they ever segregated the twins. It does mean putting manpower into it, and since it is not a local matter, we should have to charge you."

"How much?"

"Say I put a man on it, and say the job takes three days. It has to be overtime because we're pretty tight. Could you put out six pounds an hour?"

"In dollars?"

"About eleven dollars an hour."

Masuto sighed and shook his head. "Tell me something, Inspector. Why must we go to the hospitals? Don't you have a city hall of some kind in Edinburgh where every birth is noted and filed? How do you people get birth certificates for passports and that kind of thing?"

"Well, sure, lad, we have a town hall. We are not savages out here."

"Oh, no," Masuto said quickly. "I didn't mean that at all. But wouldn't they have birth records?"

"And how would you know if they were twins or not?"

"If you give me the number, I'll try."

Masuto jotted down the number and thanked the inspector and then called the operator for charges.

"Forty-two dollars and fifty cents," the operator said.

Masuto took a deep breath and then put through his call to the Town Hall at Edinburgh. He asked for birth records, and a cheerful feminine voice told him that he had reached the proper destination.

"This is Mrs. Gordon. What can I do for you?"

"My name is Masao Masuto, detective sergeant on the Beverly Hills police force. I am calling from California on a very important police matter which has to do with a homicide." He got it all out in one breath, pressured by the fact that this was the second call and he had absolutely nothing.

"How exciting! Beverly Hills!" He was becoming used to the Scottish burr and had to strain less hard to understand it. But if he had heard the accent in California, he realized, he very likely would not have known that it was Scottish.

"And your name is Japanese," Mrs. Gordon went on. "We had three seminars on Japanese influences in California and Hawaii. Absolutely fascinating. And since you have no accent except your American one, you must be a Nisei, as they say, and on the police force in Beverly Hills." Mrs. Gordon did not bother to explain the seminars, or what they were, or where they were, but plunged right on into the wonders of long distance telephoning. "Because I do hear you as clearly as if you were in the next room—"

"Mrs. Gordon," he begged her, "this is an urgent police matter."

"Of course. But before you say another word—I'm not sworn to silence, am I? I can tell my friends?"

"Absolutely. Now, here's the problem. I have to know whether in the year nineteen thirty, twins were born in Edinburgh to a woman whose name was Mackenzie."

"Would you know the twins' names?"

"One was named Robert. The name of the other I don't know."

"No problem. We file the birth proof alphabetically within each year. Oh, it might take ten minutes."

"Really. And would it take much longer for the years twenty-eight and twenty-nine?"

"A few minutes more."

"You know, Mrs. Gordon, I got through with a bit of luck. The overseas operator said it might take an hour or so, but somehow I did get right through. If we keep this connection open, do you suppose you can come up with the information in ten minutes—all three years?"

"I think so."

"I'll hang on. Go to it and bless you."

Masuto sat at his desk, phone in hand, staring at his wristwatch and hoping that Wainwright would not appear and demand to know what he was up to.

It did not take ten minutes. Nine minutes by his watch, the cheerful voice of Mrs. Gordon called him out of his reverie. "Sergeant Masuto— I am pronouncing it right, Masuto?"

"Yes, Mrs. Gordon."

"No heather on the hills, as we say. Dry run. No Mackenzie twins in twenty-eight, twenty-nine, or thirty, not a one. I have Macwortels, Stevenson, Cavendish, MacSwains—just changed on all those. But no Mackenzie twins, and we do have a lot of Mackenzies here in Edinburgh. Are you terribly disappointed?"

"Not at all," Masuto said. "It's what I expected, and you are a charming and generous lady."

The charges, Masuto learned from the operator, came to sixty-three dollars and sixty cents, and since he felt that a man must face what he must face, he went to Wainwright's office.

"How much?"

"Two calls. Forty-two dollars and fifty cents and sixty-three dollars and sixty cents."

"Two calls."

"This," Masuto said, trying to control himself, "is the richest city in the world."

"I know that. I'm not taking it out of your pay."

"Thank you."

"What did you learn?"

"The Mackenzie twins were not born in Edinburgh, unless their name was some other than Mackenzie. Not in Scotland, I'm willing to swear. Captain, you're always burned up when I say I know something and I don't have a shred of proof to back it up. I knew Mackenzie was not a Scot, but I had to have some confirmation. Sure, he could have come from Glasgow or some other Scottish city, but if he did, why lie and say Edinburgh?"

"All right, if that's what you wanted and you need it, you got your hundred dollars worth. I don't see it, but it's your case. What now?"

"Fenwick. I have to talk to Soames."

"You watch your step, Masao. There's money and power and the Pentagon involved with Fenwick. You don't play games."

"I have no death wish. I may feel guilty as hell that poor Clint died in my car, but I have no wish to join him."

"Yes, but when you go up there, Masao, you're on your own. I can't send any cops up there with you. The sheriff's department would eat my ass off. He's always screaming that his four thousand deputies are as good as any cops. That's bullshit. I wouldn't leave it to his deputies to track a diarrhea victim to an outhouse, and if the deputies miss you, there's the highway patrol." He spread his hands. "We're a small city with a handful of cops and we're surrounded."

"I'll be careful."

18

The telephone in his own office was ringing. It was Beckman, and he told Masuto that he finally got Judge Simpkins's signature on the search warrant.

"Should I head in to the Mackenzie place now, Masao?"

"No, I'd rather we did it together. Anyway, I need a little life insurance. I'm going up to see Soames at Fenwick. Give me an hour, and then drive up there and tell them you were to meet me there. If they put you off or tell you that you can't see me or tell you that I left before you got there, you raise all kinds of hell. But don't go busting in there. Get the captain on your radio and tell him what happened and then sit tight."

"You got to be crazy, Masao. Let's go in there together."

"I'm not crazy and I don't think anything's going to happen and I think they'll be as polite as punch. So just do as I say, Sy. Wait an hour and then drive up there, which will give me thirty or forty minutes with Mr. Soames."

Downstairs, the city mechanic was leaning against Masuto's borrowed Ford. "I been waiting for you, Sergeant," he said. "There are three places they're likely to put a bomb, under the hood—" he raised the engine hood "—here or here. Mostly they don't trigger it to the hood, but to the ignition, but even so, I'd raise the hood very slow, looking for wires." He then got down on his knees and pointed under the car. "Place number two—right there under your seat. And place number three, back there against the gas tank. Then you really go out in a blaze of glory. You know what I would do if I were in your shoes, Sergeant?"

"Tell me."

"You know, the people in the mob, they live with this kind of thing, so they developed a piece of mechanism small enough to fit in your pocket. You can stand a hundred feet from your car and turn on the ignition. You can buy it for forty-five bucks downtown in Meyer's Hardware, and if you ask me, the department ought to pay for it."

It had never occurred to Masuto that one could live like this for a lifetime. He thanked the mechanic and drove off. An hour later he was on the approach road to the Fenwick Works.

Begun forty years ago by Lyson Fenwick, who owned some four thousand acres of the hills to the east of Malibu Beach, the Fenwick Works was devoted at first to his dream of a plane with vertical takeoff. After Fenwick's death, the direction of the plant was switched to esoteric guidance systems, bombsights, and target-seeking missiles. The plant, a complex of white stone buildings, was situated on a high bluff, overlooking the Pacific in one direction and the canyons of the coastal range on the other. The approach road, twisting up toward the plant, reminded Masuto of pictures of medieval castles, and the twelve-foot-high chain link fence that surrounded the place and the two ten-foot guardposts that flanked the gates did nothing to lessen the feeling. Two men, dressed in the gray uniforms of private guards, each of them armed with a holstered pistol, stopped his car and asked, very politely, what his business might be.

He identified himself and said that he wished to see Mr. Soames.

"Do you have an appointment?"

"I'm afraid not."

"You're a long way from Beverly Hills," the other guard said.

"Suppose you call Mr. Soames and tell him I'm here."

The two guards stared at him, their faces blank. There are no intelligence tests for armed guards, and Masuto could almost follow their laborious attempt to figure out which would bring them the good conduct medals, roughing him up and turning him away or calling Soames's assistant, since Soames was beyond their level of direct approach. They decided for the latter and used the telephone, and then they opened the gate and told Masuto, "The big building on the left. Just park opposite and go in. Someone will meet you. Pin this on your lapel." He handed Masuto a badge while the other guard stuck a card on the Ford's windshield.

Masuto parked his car in the paved area opposite the big building that formed the center of the complex, and then he walked toward the entrance. As he approached the double doors, they opened and a pretty,

young blond woman stepped out, smiled, and informed him that he was
Sergeant Masuto. Masuto agreed with her conclusion, and nodded.

"I'm Marion Phelps, Mr. Soames's secretary. He asked me to escort
you to his office."

"That's very thoughtful of him," Masuto said.

"Mr. Soames is a very thoughtful man."

That ended their conversation. They entered the building, where
Miss Phelps smiled at an armed guard who sat at a table covered with
lights that blinked on and off, panels of switches, and two telephones;
and then they turned to the left and went through a pair of glass doors
into a room furnished in what might be called industrial modern:
leather and metal chairs and couches, chrome, and polished stainless
steel.

"If you will wait here just a moment," Miss Phelps said.

Masuto remained standing, and it was no more than a minute until
Soames appeared. He was absolutely genial. He shook hands with
Masuto. "Glad you finally turned up," he said. "I consider it an experi-
ence. Your reputation goes before you."

"We have reopened the Mackenzie case," Masuto said with stiff for-
mality.

Soames looked at his watch. He was one of those large, good-looking
men who had learned and mastered all the gradations and inflections of
graciousness, and who knew how and when to use them. "It's twelve-
forty," he said. "I usually don't lunch until one, but I'm sure you're
hungry, Sergeant, and it gives us time for one drink. We have our own
dining room here, and I don't think I'm boasting when I say that we set
the best table in southern California."

"I'm sure you do," Masuto agreed, "and I'm most grateful. But I
have luncheon plans, so why don't we use the twenty minutes to talk."

Soames regarded him thoughtfully before he said, "As you wish. My
office is through this door."

The office was large but not opulent. If anything, it was, Masuto
decided, expensively severe. On the desk, no pictures of wife or child,
and on the walls, large abstract paintings in tones of blue and gray. A
controlled man, a man who never let the situation get out of hand.
There would be no anger today, no rage, no raised voices.

"Please sit down, Sergeant," Soames said. "Do you smoke? I have
excellent Cubans, Romeo and Juliet, if you're a cigar smoker. Or a
cigarette?"

"Thank you. I don't smoke."

"And I am sure that you'd refuse a drink. Ascetics have always puzzled me."

"I'm not an ascetic. I don't drink on duty."

"Of course. Then it's not a part of being a Zen Buddhist?"

Masuto smiled. "Did you have me investigated, Mr. Soames? Do you also know my tastes in travel and women?"

"In any area that concerns us, we inform ourselves."

"Yes, I am sure. But since your time is limited, could we get to the substance of what brought me here?"

"Of course."

"You know who David Pringle is?"

"Yes. Of course. He's a theatrical lawyer who took care of poor Eve's affairs."

"I spoke to him this morning. He told me a number of things that confirmed my own conclusions. Mine were simply conclusions from scanty evidence. He spoke of what he knew. He told me that the dead man in the bathtub in the Mackenzie home was not the Mackenzie you employ but his twin brother."

"Oh?"

"You don't appear surprised. But of course you knew that."

"What else did Mr. Pringle tell you?"

"That you offered Mrs. Mackenzie fifty thousand dollars not to reveal this and to accept an indictment and trial. And incidentally, if anything happens to Mr. Pringle—well, let me simply say that we will find the perpetrator."

"That's rather dramatic, isn't it, Sergeant?"

"Did you know the body was not Robert Mackenzie?"

"Yes, we knew."

"Where was Mr. Mackenzie?"

"He was in Canada the night his brother was murdered, so he could not have been involved."

"Where in Canada?" Masuto demanded.

"I can't tell you that."

"Why was he in Canada?"

"I can't tell you that either. It has nothing to do with this matter."

"I think it has."

"That's your privilege, Sergeant."

"Did you offer Mrs. Mackenzie fifty thousand dollars to stand trial?"

"Of course not. Think about it, Sergeant. It's absolutely absurd."

"Then Pringle was lying?"

Soames leaned back in his chair and stared at Masuto thoughtfully.

Then he spread his hands. "All right, but this is confidential, sir, on your honor as a gentleman. Anyway, the poor woman's dead. Eve Mackenzie was a hopeless alcoholic, but the kind of alcoholic who could go about things and give the appearance of being cold sober. She always moved very slowly, which gave her an appearance of great dignity. Now, she could tell her lawyer or anyone else anything, invent anything. You're not surprised?"

"I knew she was an alcoholic."

"That answers your question."

Masuto shook his head. "Hardly. Tell me, Mr. Soames, did you know that Robert Mackenzie's name was not Robert Mackenzie and that he was not born in Edinburgh?"

Soames looked at his watch. "Just one o'clock, Sergeant. Are you sure you won't break bread with us?"

"I think not."

"Do you know, Sergeant," Soames said, "a wise man knows when to stop asking questions. A wise man knows when a nuisance becomes an impediment. Don't press your luck."

"That's not a threat, is it?"

Soames laughed. "Would I engage in threats? Sergeant, even a man so experienced as yourself falls into the trap of believing the nonsense one sees in films and on television. We don't eliminate people and we don't kill people. When I asked you not to press your luck, I simply meant that overreaching could have unpleasant consequences in terms of your employment, pension plan—that sort of thing."

"But, you see, I am lucky. In the past three days there have been two attempts to kill me, and I survived both."

"Yes, I know about that. I assure you, we had nothing to do with either of those stupid acts. If I should find it necessary to take some action—ah, but why talk that way? Why not let the whole thing drop? What's done is done. I think that's a good Zen position—the moment is now, and that is all that matters."

"For action," Masuto said. "Not for memory."

"You refuse to lunch with us. In any case, I would like you to stay here this afternoon. There are people coming from Washington whom I would like you to meet."

"I'm afraid not this afternoon. I have work to do."

"I think you must stay, Sergeant. I was asked to have you here. I don't think you should make a scene. It's only for a few hours."

The door to his office opened and two armed guards stepped into the room. At the same time, the telephone on Soames's desk rang. Soames picked up the telephone, listened, and said, "He's on his way." Then he turned to Masuto. "You do have a way with you, Sergeant. There's an oversized man standing at our gate who claims to be a Beverly Hills detective and who is holding his gun to the throat of one of our guards, and who says that if you don't walk out of here in the next five minutes, he'll have to shoot the guard. Now, that's a little outrageous and totally uncalled for. Please get over there and put an end to it."

The two guards escorted Masuto out more hurriedly than he had entered. He got into his car without recalling the city mechanic's advice about the bomb and drove to the gate. The gate was open. On the outside, Beckman was holding a guard by his shirt front, half off the ground, the muzzle of Beckman's revolver pressing against the underside of the man's chin. Three other guards, shotguns pointed at Beckman, stood around the two.

"Go down the road," Beckman shouted to Masuto.

Masuto drove down to the access road, stopped, got out of his car, and turned around. Beckman shouted to the shotgun guards, "I'm taking this baby down to the main road. He can walk back from there." He herded him into his car and then said to him, "You behave while I'm driving or I'll break your neck. I need only one hand for that."

19

They had lunch at Alice's Restaurant on the Malibu Pier, two tall men, one heavy and slope-shouldered, the other slender and wiry, each noticing the other's hand still shook a bit. Beckman had a hamburger. Masuto had cold fish. It was tasteless, but then anything would have been tasteless the way he felt. He had eaten here in the past with Kati and the children. The food had always been very good.

"It's me," he muttered, pushing the plate away.

"I know," Beckman said, but he went on eating. "Masao, what was that all about?"

"I don't know," Masuto said slowly. "I just don't know. I think I'm beginning to get a glimmer, and then it's turned on its head. We never had anything like this before."

"What do you suppose they planned to do with you up there at Fenwick?"

"Nothing. I think they had some brass coming up from Washington, and they were going to put the heat on me with no holds barred. Nothing physical, but I think they felt that if they had me there, they could talk me into dropping the investigation—or maybe threaten and frighten me into it. But why? Why are they so damned eager to close the case and to make the world forget that a man was killed who was Mackenzie's twin brother?"

"Masao, who are they? Who are we up against?"

"I don't know that either. I think it's the C.I.A., and then I have to ask myself, why would the C.I.A. want me dead? I don't put it past them, but why? No, it's not that simple, and it's not just Fenwick and the C.I.A., and where's Mackenzie, who isn't Mackenzie, and I don't think he's a Scot either."

"What makes you say that?"

"Well, I called Edinburgh this morning and discovered that no Mackenzie twins were born in the possible years. But what intrigues me a lot more is that I spoke to three different Scots, two men and two women, not to mention the local operators. The accent is fascinating. I mean it sounds a bit German, a bit Dutch. First time I ever really listened to—I mean listened from a certain point of view. Didn't you once tell me that you have a psychiatrist in the family?"

"Sarah's side of the family. They're the intellectuals who regard me as a dumb cop. Her cousin, Alvin Shapiro. Nice guy. Whenever I see him, which is at weddings, bar mitzvahs, and funerals, he's got a whole list of questions about being a cop."

"Do you suppose he'd answer a question or two for me? From what I hear, they keep a ten-minute spot between patients. Where's his office?"

"On Camden."

"Good. We can hit it on our way over to the Mackenzie house. Suppose you call him now."

A few minutes later, Beckman returned to the table and informed Masuto that Dr. Alvin Shapiro would see them at exactly ten minutes to four. "And when he says exactly, he means it."

"It's all right—just about as much time as we need. Give me the address, and I'll meet you outside the building."

Dr. Alvin Shapiro's office had a couch, leather with a headrest. There were also two armchairs and a desk, and blinds muted the room to soft lamplight, even though the sun still shone outside. Dr. Shapiro was five feet five inches on top of three-inch heels, an alert birdlike man with the brightest blue eyes Masuto had ever seen. He shook hands with them eagerly. "So you're Sy's partner. Heard a great deal about you. You have a fan there. According to Sy, you're a cross between Sam Spade and Mr. Moto."

Masuto burst out laughing. "That is delightful—Sam Spade and Mr. Moto."

"Who the hell is Mr. Moto?" Beckman wanted to know.

"A pre–World War II creation of J. P. Marquand. But let's get down to your question. A Beverly Hills psychiatrist is a prisoner of time and greed. What can I do for you?"

"About brothers," Masuto said, "fratricide, the ancient Cain and Abel syndrome, how common is it?"

"There's a name for it. It happens."

"But compared to matricide or patricide?"

"Ah—there you've put your finger on an interesting fact. I was just reading a statistical study of this last month. Fratricide is much less common. It would almost appear that the link between brothers, or brother and sister, or sisters is deeper than between parent and child. But that kind of thinking can also be deceptive, since parent and child are separated by a generation gap and very often by a large cultural gap —neither of which would be present in a sibling relationship. Sibling jealousy and rivalry play another kind of a role."

"I see. Now tell me about twins, if you would."

"Identical twins or fraternal twins?"

"Identical twins. How likely is the cold-blooded murder—not rage and anger, but cold-blooded murder of one twin by another?"

"Premeditated and deliberate? I presume you are discussing an actual case, Sergeant, and that you didn't come here for an instructive dialogue."

"An actual case."

"How old are these twins?"

"Fifty-three."

"You know, Sergeant, identical twins are one of the great psychological mysteries of our profession. If I were to wax somewhat poetic, I might describe such twins as the appearance of one soul divided between two bodies. The syndrome is absolutely fascinating. Do you know, there have been cases of such twins separated as small children, living their lives a continent apart, never seeing each other, yet choosing identical professions and wives who were enough alike to look like sisters, and even choosing the same type of house to live in. It brings up all sorts of absolutely fascinating speculations, and I think that if I were really loaded, I'd take off two or three years and devote them to the study of identical twins. But you were talking about murder, cold-blooded, deliberate murder."

"Yes, murder."

Shapiro scratched his head and wrinkled his brow. "Do you know, Sergeant, I've never heard of such a case. That doesn't mean it hasn't happened. It could have happened any number of times, and my reading is limited. No—if it had happened with any kind of frequency, one of the journals would have written it up. You know, such a murder would be more difficult to undertake than suicide. The murderer would destroy the non-participating self."

"But it could happen?"

"Sergeant, anything can happen. I simply feel that it is very unlikely, very unlikely indeed."

Masuto stood up and thanked him.

"On the other hand," Dr. Shapiro said, "since I've given you at least fifty dollars worth of Beverly Hills shrink time on the cuff, I want in return the privilege of taking both of you to lunch when this is all over and hearing the solution."

"Be glad to lunch with you," Masuto said glumly, "but as to a solution—"

"There'll be a solution," Beckman promised him.

Downstairs, Masuto said to Beckman, "What makes you think so?"

"I know you."

"I liked your cousin. He's no fool."

"Except," Beckman said, "that I had Mackenzie absolutely pegged for the killing of his brother."

"No, it made no sense. I wanted some way to get him off that mental hook, and your cousin gave it to me. Feona Scott killed the twin, Feona and Mr. X. Why all the Scots? Who helped her? It wasn't Soames—that makes no sense at all. Sy, you have the search warrants?"

"Right here in my pocket."

"All right. We'll drive over to the Mackenzie house. If the lovely Feona is there, I'm going to arrest her for the murder of the twin."

"Come on, Masao. You told me I had no case against Eve. What kind of a case do you have against Feona?"

"I'll put something together. She had access to the notebook. She was there when it happened."

"And what was her motive?"

"When I find Mackenzie—"

"For God's sake, Masuto, this thing is getting to you. If you arrest her, they'll have her out in ten minutes flat. I've never seen you like this before."

"She's the key to it. Look at me, Sy, I've sent my wife and kids away, I keep looking over my shoulder, Clint died in my car—and right there —there's your car and there's mine. Did you get a neat set of instructions on how to look for a bomb in your car?"

"I got them."

"All right. Let's see if our cars are clean. If they are, I'll meet you at the Mackenzie place."

Lexington Road, about a mile in length, begins at Sunset Boulevard, goes north, and then curves west to end at a street called Whittier, and in this rather short distance displays some of the most expensive real estate in the world. There is probably no house on Lexington Road that could be bought for less than a million dollars, and there are a good many houses that would fetch well over two million dollars. The Mackenzie house was somewhere in between, a big two-story white house in what was loosely called the Mediterranean style.

Beckman had just gotten out of his car when Masuto's car pulled up and parked next to his. A large curving driveway in front of the house bent in the middle to provide an area where a dozen cars could be comfortably parked, and from this point a wide path led into the house. Beckman wondered by what virtue Feona Scott continued to occupy the premises, and Masuto thought it was simply a matter of not allowing the house to stay empty.

"Even here in Beverly Hills, an empty house is a provocation."

"But she was here while Eve was still alive."

"Eve Mackenzie was not very alive. She was a drunk, Sy. She couldn't be alone."

"And who owns the house now?"

"That's hard to say. It may be Eve's sister, if Mackenzie made a will to favor Eve. Maybe when we have enough time to breathe and can stop running, I'll explain the whole thing. Meanwhile, let's face the good Feona."

"Are you really going to bust her?"

"I am."

"And you're sure she killed the twin?"

"She and someone else, so ring the bell and let's get on with it."

Beckman pressed the bell button. It was one of those electric chime affairs, and the chimes sounded simultaneously all over the house. It was a strange arrangement, but logical where the occupant was an alcoholic, and standing in front of the house, Masuto could hear the tinkling sound behind every window. But there was no sound of anyone stirring inside the house.

"Try again," he told Beckman. The tinkling sounded once more.

"Looks like she's out."

"Let's have a shot at the lock," Masuto said.

"Breaking and entering?"

"There's a Westinghouse alarm system, but it's turned off. Either she's careless or she doesn't give a damn. As far as this lock is concerned, a hungry wolf could blow his way through it." Masuto took out of his pocket a key ring without keys. Instead, four oddly shaped pieces of metal were hooked on to it. He selected one of the metal probes, worked it into the lock, and then worked the door handle. The door opened.

"We could have waited," Beckman said uneasily.

"Maybe not."

"What does that mean?"

"We'll see. Go upstairs, Sy. I'll take the downstairs."

"What am I looking for?"

"I don't know exactly—photographs, papers, passports, a wall safe, books that don't fit—shake the books. A book can have a lot in it that isn't printed."

"I'm with you."

"See if there's an attic entrance."

"Right."

Beckman started up the stairs and Masuto went into the library, a room facing him on his left. Unlike Beckman, he had never been in the Mackenzie house before. There were many Japanese—Niseis too—who believed, as the Chinese did, that the ghosts of those who died in a house were trapped there for years after. Of course, there are Westerners who believe the same thing, but Masuto heard many stories of rich Hong Kong Chinese, eager for a foothold in Los Angeles, who would buy only new houses. Himself, he deplored superstition, but from the moment he had set foot in this house, he had sensed a miasma that made his skin prickle and tightened his muscles. He went into the library with the same tense alertness with which a hunter might step into the jungle, and as he studied the wall of books, he heard Beckman's shout.

"Masao! Up here!"

He took the steps three at a time. A man who shouts like that could be in desperate trouble, but it was with more muted tones that Beckman called him into the big master bedroom.

"I'm here—in the bathroom, Masao."

He joined Beckman in the bathroom. In the bathtub, which was empty of water, Feona Scott was sitting. She was stark naked, and two thin streams of dried blood ran down her face from a bullet hole square in the middle of her forehead.

20

"It is now four forty-five P.M.," Dr. Baxter, who enjoyed being specific, announced. "I make it some time this morning—anywhere from eight to ten hours ago."

"I found her clothes," Beckman announced from his position under the bed. Somehow he had squeezed himself under there. Now he was trying to work his way out.

For the third time, Brody, the firearms expert, asked Baxter when he could have the bullet.

"You don't hear, do you? You don't listen, you don't hear. You have as much brains as your colleague over there, Mr. Sweeney, crawling around and trying to pick up fingerprints."

"You give me a pain in the ass," Sweeney said.

"Look, Doc, I was only pushing because I got a theory. I got a theory that hole in her head was made by a thirty caliber. Now, that's not a usual caliber, thirty."

Beckman, spreading her clothes on the bed, said, "I will be damned. These were ripped off her."

"She is stacked," Brody said.

"What are you, some kind of ghoul?" Beckman demanded.

"He's a dimwitted necrophile. But in a cop, nothing surprises me," Dr. Baxter snorted. "Where's Wainwright?"

"Downstairs with the sergeant," Brody said.

"Don't keep staring at her. What is with you characters—haven't you ever seen a naked woman before? Get a robe or a blanket or something and cover her up."

"Where?"

"In the closet, you lackluster moron."

Beckman went to the closet with Brody. "Don't mind him. He hates these things," he whispered to Brody. "I think it scares him. All he wants is to stay in the pathology lab in the basement of All Saints Hospital and cut people who have died of ordinary causes like screwed-up operations."

"Cover her up," Baxter said. "I'm going downstairs to talk to the brain trust."

"What's a necrophile?" Brody asked him.

"What!"

"What's to get sore about? I'm no doctor. How should I know what a necrophile is?"

"Eat more fish. It's good for the brain." As he started down the stairs, Beckman called after him, "Tell the sergeant I found her clothes."

Officer Keller was at the bottom of the stairs, and Baxter said to him, "Where are they?"

"In the kitchen."

The kitchen was a large room, twenty feet by twenty feet, festooned as were most kitchens in Beverly Hills with the newest wonders in stoves, refrigerators, and small kitchen appliances. Wainwright and Masuto sat at a big butcher-block table, drinking coffee. On the table was a large brown purse, its contents spread out across one end of the table.

"Have a cup of coffee," Wainwright said.

"What is with you people? Up there, Brody comments on how stacked this Feona Scott was, and now you two sit here drinking coffee."

"Why not?"

"Why not? Why not? This is a house in which a murder took place."

"You're a medical examiner, not a damn preacher," Wainwright said.

"Then pay me what a medical examiner should be paid. You got the excuse that nothing happens in Beverly Hills to require a full-time medical examiner. Then what's that upstairs? You'll soon have them dropping out of the trees."

"It's just instant coffee," Masuto said gently, "two spoonfuls. The water stays hot in that cooler affair. You see, it's got two—"

"I know what it is. No thank you."

"When was she killed?"

"Between seven-thirty and eight-thirty this morning. Your brilliant Brody thinks it was a thirty-caliber bullet, but he's wrong, and anyone who makes a mistake like that shouldn't pose as any kind of an expert. But what can you expect of Rexford Drive?" naming the street where the combined City Hall–police station was located.

"What did kill her?" Wainwright asked respectfully.

"Twenty-two short. Far enough away to leave no powder marks and expertly placed. I'm no arms expert, but I'd say the man carries a semiautomatic, one of those magazine things that spray bullets."

"Yet he used only one bullet," Masuto said.

"He's good. Well, I'm taking off now. I'll send the ambulance for the body. Do you want an autopsy?"

"Will it reveal anything?" Masuto asked. "I saw no needle marks. Do you think she was a doper?"

"No reason to think so. What about it, Captain?"

"I don't know. You're specifying the cause of death. What do you think, Masao?"

"I think she was shot and killed, and that's it."

"Then skip it," Wainwright said.

"All right. But what about the body?"

"Put it in a cold locker."

"We got just so many cold lockers. I have to fill in a report for the hospital and tell them just how long that locker will be occupied—for which, I may remind you, they charge us twenty dollars a day. Now what is with this Feona Scott? Does she have a relative?"

"There was some talk that she was Mackenzie's mistress. And having seen her in her birthday suit, I can believe it. And I'll tell you something else. There is nobody we'd rather talk to right now than Mr. Robert Mackenzie, but where he is, God only knows."

"We're trying to find some connection with Feona Scott," Masuto told him, "so just put her on ice for a few days and then we'll see."

"As you say, as you say. By the way, your oversized snoop upstairs says he found her clothes." With that, Baxter departed.

"So what do we have?" Wainwright asked.

Masuto pointed to the contents of the purse. "A hundred and sixteen dollars. A lot of cash for a housekeeper to carry. Small checkbook for an account at Crocker. Balance—nine hundred and twelve dollars, fourteen cents. Checks very normal, cash checks mostly under one hundred dollars, check to Ralph's supermarket, check to Thrifty drugstore, check to Robinson's. Driver's license. Social security card—tell me, Captain. Suppose we put this card on the wire to Washington. They must be computerized, so they could give us the facts, where she was born, et cetera."

"No problem. But they're three hours later on the time belts, so it'll have to wait for tomorrow."

"Yes. Keller!" Masuto called.

"Yes, sir?" the officer asked, coming into the kitchen.

"Would you go upstairs and ask Beckman to come down and bring the clothes with him."

"What clothes?"

"He'll know."

Keller departed and Dr. Baxter returned and said, "Something I forgot to tell you, thought you'd like to know."

"Oh?"

"About the cadaver that was Eve Mackenzie."

"What about it?"

"Well, her sister came and signed for it and had it shipped over to a funeral home for cremation."

"That's what you came back to tell us?" Wainwright demanded sourly.

"No."

"Then what in hell are you talking about?"

"Thought you'd be interested in who was with her."

"Mark Geffner?" Masuto asked softly.

"What!"

Wainwright burst into laughter.

"How did you know that?" Baxter asked, chagrined.

"We have ways. No, we're grateful to you, Doc, really. Tell me something before you leave. What did the man in the tub die from—the man they thought was Mackenzie?" Wainwright was being very polite for Wainwright.

"Cardiac arrest."

"What does that mean?"

"It means his heart stopped beating. What do you think it means?"

At that point, Beckman came into the kitchen, carrying the clothes. He paused at the door, behind the doctor.

"But you specified electrocution as the cause of death," Masuto said.

"Now, wait a red-hot minute, my Oriental wonder. You were in Japan when the man was killed, which was two months ago, and now you sit there and tell me I specified death by electrocution!"

Masuto turned to Beckman. "Sy, didn't you tell me that Doc here made a determination?"

"I think I told you the twin was electrocuted, but I don't think I said that Dr. Baxter made the determination."

"Well, did you?" Masuto asked Baxter.

"Did I what?"

"Specify electrocution, or the blow on the head? You keep changing your diagnosis."

"Does it matter now?" Wainwright asked. Baxter's fits of spleen always made him nervous.

"Yes, it matters," Masuto insisted.

"I told you what I determined to be the cause of his death. Cardiac arrest. What happened that night killed him, but whether it was the blow to his head severe enough to fracture his skull or electrocution, I don't know. I wasn't there."

"Then there was no way to discover whether he had been electrocuted or not?" Masuto asked.

"His body wasn't burned—no, no way."

"So the whole electrocution thing might have been a scene set to direct attention away?"

"Could be."

"Away from where?" Wainwright asked.

"I'm not sure, not yet."

"And I'm going home," Baxter said, shaking his head hopelessly and stamping out of the room.

"What eats him?" Wainwright wondered.

"I don't know that anything eats him. I think he just enjoys being the way he is." He gave the social security card to Wainwright, swept everything else back into the purse, put the purse on a counter, and said to Beckman, "Bring the clothes over here, Sy, and let's spread them out on this tabletop. By the way, where were they?"

"Just pushed under the bed."

"Interesting," Masuto said to Wainwright. "Last time, the twin's clothes disappeared—never found, just as his body disappeared. Both told a story they didn't want us to read."

"Not this time."

"No, indeed," Masuto said, spreading the bundle of clothes. "Look at this, Captain. Cotton dress, ripped open from the neck down—great anger. Here—this is a blood spot, so she was dead already when he undressed her. Tore the clothes off her, I should say."

"Why?"

"It's a reprise, Captain. She killed his brother and then put the dead man through the ridiculous indignity of sitting dead and naked in a bathtub."

"Mackenzie? You're saying that the real Mackenzie killed her?"

"No question about it as far as I'm concerned. No proof yet, no evidence, but I'm ready to go out on a limb."

"That still leaves one loose end," Beckman said. He held up a bronze statuette about two inches in diameter and ten inches high, Atlas holding the earth as a globe above his head. "I found this in the library or den or whatever you call it. The legs make an easy grip, and the globe acts like it was meant for a sap. I don't know what else she could have used, and I can't find anything that she maybe just picked up and sapped him with. So what I mean is that if she did that downstairs, there's no way in the world that lady could have gotten the twin upstairs and into the bathtub."

"You're right. No way," Masuto agreed.

"That leaves a place open," Wainwright said. "If it wasn't Mackenzie."

"If it were Mackenzie," Masuto said, "then the scene in the bathroom upstairs is absolutely senseless. I don't think it's senseless. I don't think Mackenzie had anything to do with killing his brother—except possibly in a roundabout way. He was spelling out his revenge brutally and dangerously when he put Feona into the bathtub. But he wasn't talking to us. He was talking to the third party—the man who helped Feona kill the twin and drag the body upstairs."

"Masao," Wainwright said with annoyance, "I've watched you spin out these guesses of yours too many times not to put a lot of faith in them. But this time we're not playing parlor games. One of my men is dead. We're going to his funeral tomorrow. And that was the second attempt to kill you."

"I was aware of that."

"Don't get cool on me. Nobody's that cool. Who was the man with Feona?"

"I don't know."

"You're lying."

"That's flattering, Captain. I wish I had the crystal ball you credit me with. I don't. I don't know who was with Feona that night. I don't know why they killed the twin. I think I could make twenty wild guesses, but what good is that? You could do the same, Sy could do the same. I don't know why they wanted to kill me. I don't know who wanted to kill me."

Beckman had wandered out of the room during this. Sweeney and Brody came down and stood in the kitchen entrance.

"I got everything," Sweeney said. "Can I go?"

"Have you got the dead woman's prints?" Masuto asked him.

"What?"

"I said, do you have the prints of that woman in the bathtub upstairs?"

"Do you want them?"

"Officer Sweeney," Masuto said deliberately, "do you remember that I was rather provoked with you when you told me you didn't have Mackenzie's prints?"

"Sergeant, I told you it was not procedure."

"Sweeney," Wainwright roared, "get your ass upstairs and take a set of prints from the woman in the tub! Both hands! Perfect!"

"Nothing more I can do upstairs," Officer Brody said as Sweeney hurried past him.

"Take a post at the door—outside."

"What's a necrophile?"

"A what?"

"Fascination with dead bodies," Masuto told him.

"You're kidding."

"No, that's what it means."

Brody walked away, shaking his head, and Beckman came back and announced, "They're here."

"The media. There's a CBS sound truck outside, and there's a young kid from the *L.A. Times.*"

"That's the beginning. What do you think, Masao? Should we talk to them?"

"There's no way in the world you can keep a lid on it now. Two naked dead bodies in the same tub two months apart, one a man, one a woman. It has to be the juiciest bit of kinky madness that they've had to play with in a long time. You can hint that it's a copycat murder that some lunatic put together, but the trouble is there's no sign of breaking and entering."

"I put in a call for Abramson an hour ago," Wainwright said. "I wish to hell I knew what the public relations implications of this are. Today a cop can't just be a cop, and especially in Beverly Hills."

Masuto looked at his watch. "It's seven o'clock. I think the evening is just beginning."

"That's instructive. What in hell do I say?"

"I don't know. You called Mr. Abramson." Masuto shook his head. "Until he comes and decides how he wants to handle this, I say nothing."

"What's nothing?"

"Just no comment."

"The ambulance is here for the body," Beckman announced.

"Beckman—I want those All Saints people to keep their mouths shut," Wainwright told him.

"I'll try, but they'll blab. They been pushing Officer Garcia out front, and he let out that it's a murder."

"You tell him one more word out of him or anyone else and I'll burn their asses good and plenty."

"Did you call about the alarm?" Masuto asked Beckman.

"Never turned on."

"He had a key. He could have let himself in or she could have let him in."

"Where do you suppose he's been these two months?"

"According to Soames, Canada."

"Doing what?"

"Heaven only knows," Masuto said. "Sy, in the original investigation, did it come out what kind of engineer Mackenzie was?"

"Chemical engineer. His specialty was missile fuel."

"Fascinating."

Beckman left to spell out the law of silence to the cops outside. The ambulance people came down the stairs carrying Feona Scott's remains, and Abramson, the city manager, was let in by Beckman and brought to the kitchen.

"Just tell me whether what I hear is true?"

"Do you want a cup of coffee?"

"How about a stiff Scotch?"

"It's in the library," Masuto said, "but I don't think drinking his Scotch goes with the territory."

"What did you hear?" Wainwright asked him.

"Well, the poop is that this is another Manson affair, that a gang busted in, broke up the place, and disemboweled the housekeeper."

"It's kinky but not that kinky," Wainwright said. "Masuto and Beckman came here with a search warrant signed by Judge Simpkins, all very aboveboard and legal, and they found the housekeeper dead in the bathtub."

"I'll be damned. Electrocuted?"

"Shot through the head and naked."

"Well, I will be damned. Was it a break-in? Was the door open?"

Wainwright turned to Masuto. "Was it open?"

Masuto shrugged. "No. Truth is, I picked the lock."

"Naked and in the bathtub. What in God's name does that mean?"

Masuto told him what it meant, spelling out his entire theory and trusting that Wainwright would be sufficiently distracted to forget about illegal entry. He was. He listened to the recitation, and then said bleakly, "So that's what we got—the kind of thing that'll boost the circulation of the *National Enquirer* through the sky."

"I needed this!" Abramson complained. "I needed this like a hole in the head. Why can't they do these things in Pasadena or in Palos Verdes or in Bel-Air if they want a fancy neighborhood? We run a quiet city, we don't push people around, we offer a decent place to live—oh, Lord, I want to put my head on the table and weep—unless you're putting me on. Naked in the bathtub with a bullet in her head—you're not putting me on?"

"That's it," Masuto said.

"Well, we have to figure out how to handle this. We've had enough bad publicity. I can't repeat that story you told me. It's just too insane. What happened two months ago was bad enough."

Wainwright turned to Masuto. "Come on, Masao, give us something."

"It's not that much of a problem. The housekeeper, living here alone, was shot by an intruder and killed. That's all you have to say."

"And when they come up with the story about the bathtub?"

"You know nothing about any bathtub. We can keep our own men quiet, and if you talk to Baxter, he can put a lid on the ambulance people."

"It might just work."

"Worth a try."

"Where are you going, Masao?" Wainwright asked him.

"I, Honorable Captain, am going to pack it in. I'm going outside and examine my car and see whether some demented idiot placed a bomb in it, and then when I prove to myself that I will not be blown up, I shall drive through the San Fernando Valley to where my Uncle Toda grows oranges and lives like a normal human being. I shall see my wife and children, who are refugees there, since I consider my home in Culver City unsafe, and I shall eat some excellent Japanese food and sleep like a baby, guarded by several intelligent German shepherds. More intelligent than most people. Saner, too."

"You won't forget the funeral—ten o'clock?"

"I'll be there."

Wainwright turned to the city manager, who nodded. "I'll be there, Captain."

"And in uniform," Wainwright said to Masuto. "And that goes for you too, Beckman. I want you both in uniform."

"Captain," Beckman said, "I gained twenty pounds. I can't get into my uniform."

"Then either lose the twenty pounds or open the seams."

"Yes, thank you."

Masuto walked with him to the door. "Tomorrow, Sy," he said, "I want you with me all day, and then I want you to stay over at my house. Can you manage it?"

"Culver City?"

"It's the only one I have."

"She won't believe me, but I'll manage."

"See you tomorrow."

"Drive carefully."

21

Masuto felt increasingly foolish each time he looked under his car; nevertheless, he went through the routine of checking it out for bombs. He tried to form a picture in his mind of this man who wanted so persistently to kill him, but the picture eluded him. The only factor he felt reasonably sure of was that he was dealing with a professional. In that case, someone had hired him. But who?

He had to know and he had to end this. He was a sensitive man. No one thought of policemen as sensitive men, but so many of them were. Even if he could go on living with the constant threat of death, he could not endure a life where Kati and his two children lived under the same threat.

Absorbed in these thoughts, Masuto had turned into Coldwater Canyon to cross over the pass into the Valley. The rush hour, the bumper-to-bumper flood of cars out of Los Angeles and over the Coldwater pass to the endless rows of tract homes in the Valley, was over. Coldwater had become quiet again, and in this quiet, with only an occasional car in front of him and behind him, Masuto began to feel that he was being followed.

For most of the distance between Beverly Hills and the San Fernando Valley, Coldwater Canyon is a two-lane road, with no way for one car to pass another, and in the deepening twilight, accentuated in the cleft of the canyon, it was not possible for Masuto to support his feeling. The car directly behind him was a Cadillac Seville, driven by a woman, he thought, and in any case a pro would not tailgate him. The car behind that appeared to be a Mustang, but he could not get a clear enough look at it to infer anything about the driver. But once over the mountain and out of the narrow, twisting road, it was four lanes to Ventura Boulevard, and now the Cadillac pulled into the right-hand lane and the Mustang took its place behind him. It was almost dark now and the Mustang had its lights on. His rearview mirror gave Masuto no image of the man behind the wheel, and he was inclined to dismiss his suspicions as the product of an active imagination.

The light on Ventura Boulevard changed, and Masuto drove north on Coldwater Canyon Boulevard. The Mustang followed, but that was reasonable, Masuto decided. It made sense that anyone coming over Coldwater at this time of night would make for the Coldwater Canyon entrance to the Ventura Freeway, going either left toward the Valley neighborhoods or right toward Hollywood. Since Masuto intended to do neither of these but to drive past the freeway before turning left and then right on Woodman Avenue, he was grateful that here he could dispense with his suspicion.

But the Mustang did not go into either entrance to the freeway. It continued north after Masuto, remaining fifty yards behind him. When he increased his speed, the Mustang increased its speed; when he slowed, the Mustang slowed.

There was a street ahead of him that Masuto remembered, where the road ran for a quarter of a mile through a mesquite tract that had been in litigation for years and thereby undeveloped. Masuto turned his car into this street, slowing to ten miles an hour. When he saw the Mustang make the same turn, put on its bright lights, and increase its speed, Masuto braked to a stop and opened his door. As the Mustang came to a screeching stop alongside his car, Masuto rolled out of his seat and through the open door onto the ground. Simultaneously, two barrels of a sawed-off shotgun smashed into the driver's seat of the Ford Masuto had been driving, and one barrel fired immediately after the other.

Masuto moved with the speed of a snake striking, rolling over onto his feet, racing around the back of his car, and coming between the two cars after the second barrel had been discharged. The nose of the sawed-off shotgun still protruded from the open window of the Mustang, and Masuto grabbed it and yanked it toward him with all his strength. A yell of pain from the man in the driver's seat told Masuto that he had probably broken the man's trigger finger, a supposition that was confirmed later. Masuto flung the gun away, opened the door, and grabbed the wrist of the man's left hand, which held an automatic pistol, the safety catch of which he was trying to release. With both hands Masuto twisted the wrist sharply. He heard the bone snap and the gunman screamed in pain, yelling, "You mother fucker, you broke my wrist! You lousy yellow bastard, you broke my finger and you broke my wrist."

"And I'll break your neck if you don't shut up," Masuto said, dragging him out of the car. "Stand up!" The man was lean, well-dressed, about five foot ten, blond, blue-eyed. "Turn around and put your hands behind you!" Masuto cuffed him.

"Goddamn you, you put that cuff on a broken wrist. I can't stand it. My finger's bleeding. I need a bandage. I could bleed to death."

"The world could just endure the loss. Now, I am arresting you, and I am making a statement of your rights. What follows is an admonition of your rights—"

"Are you crazy? I need a doctor."

It sounded crazy to Masuto, standing there on that dark deserted road and saying, "You have the right to remain silent. If you give up the right to remain silent, anything you say can and will be held against you in a court of law. You have the right to speak with an attorney and have the attorney present during questioning—"

"Shut up! Shut up! Shut up!"

But Masuto went on, calmly reciting until done. "Whereupon, I arrest you for the murder of Oscar Clint—"

"Who the hell is Oscar Clint?"

"The man who died in my car. And I arrest you for the attempted murder of Masao Masuto. Now, move."

The two shotgun blasts had left Masuto's car a ragged mess of broken glass. Masuto put the gunman in the Mustang, where he whimpered and pleaded that his wrist hurt. He got in next to him, in the driver's seat, and said quietly, "I want to concentrate on my driving. If you interfere with me in any way or make sounds that are intolerable, I will kill you. You are a professional hired assassin, so you must know that the act is not too difficult. In my case, since I am a karate expert, I will do it, if you provoke me, with a blow to your throat, which will crush your windpipe and give you a slow, lingering death."

"What the hell are you, some kind of crazy Chinese spook?"

"I don't like my driving interfered with."

"You got me cuffed behind. I'm leaning against a broken wrist and a finger bleeding all over my car seat."

"You won't have much use for the car," Masuto assured him, wondering how he could even invent that kind of bestial threat. He decided that he was not meditating enough, that he was falling too readily into the spell that violence and fear had cast over the country, losing the thought that even this sick, depraved specimen was human. It was too

easy to fall into that, and when the pressure of this case eased up, ten or
fifteen hours of *seshin* meditation would be called for, meditation that
went on hour after hour and which would, if he were fortunate, restore
his membership in the human race.

His voice was less harsh when he asked the gunman his name.

"Suck off, you bastard."

Masuto shrugged, and wondered whether he would actually kill the
man if he tried a violent move—or was it simply an empty threat?

At the Beverly Hills police station, Masuto had to help him out of the
car. His finger had stopped bleeding but he insisted that the pain of his
wrist was killing him. Masuto marched him inside and up the stairs and
told Officer Purdy, who had night watch, to lock him in a holding cell.
Sergeant Cooper was at the night desk, and he asked Masuto what he
had there.

"I think I have the man who killed Oscar Clint."

"No! You're kidding."

"It looks damn like it. He tried to kill me tonight. He emptied both
barrels of a sawed-off shotgun into the rental Ford I was driving and put
it out of commission. Luckily, I could take him. I broke his wrist, so
you'll have to call Doc Baxter and persuade him over here."

"He'll be sore as hell. He'll take my head off. We could call the
paramedics."

"I'd rather have Baxter."

"Masuto, I hope to God it was a righteous arrest and that you read
him his rights."

"I did."

"Then why don't we book him?"

"Because I arrested him in Los Angeles. We were down in the Valley."

"Oh, no."

"Yes, and where do we stand? I think we can book him, but I'm not
certain. That's why I want to get Wainwright over here, and I want
Sweeney here too, just in case the L.A. cops come for him. I want his
prints. He won't give his name."

"If the captain can't make it, do we call anyone else?"

"No, and for the moment I don't want any of the media in on this.
My car's out in the Valley, shot to pieces and full of broken glass, and
first crack of dawn, someone's going to see it and report it to the L.A.
cops."

"You're entitled to hot pursuit wherever it takes you."

"I thought of that. Trouble is, he was in pursuit of me, and while I might fake it for a while, the L.A. cops are bound to ask why I was chasing him."

When a tired and provoked Wainwright got there, and when Masuto had repeated his story, the captain's annoyance vanished and he shook his hand heartily. "There's my blessing, Masao. If this is the loathsome son of a bitch who blew up Oscar Clint and tried to kill you, then this is one good day. But why didn't you call the L.A. cops and let them make the collar?"

"Because there's no way they'd just hand him over to me and say, take him home and question him, Sergeant Masuto, and when you and Captain Wainwright have no more use for him, you can give him back to us. You know that. They'd take him downtown and book him and work him over and if what he came up with interacted with our murder yesterday, they'd inform us, but they might also inform the C.I.A. and the Justice Department."

"Sooner or later, we'll have to hand him over."

"After we talk to him."

"Masao, do you think he killed Feona?"

"Oh, no. Absolutely not." He had considered the possibility that Feona had employed him. "Believe me, Captain, there is absolutely no doubt in my mind. Mackenzie killed Feona. But that doesn't mean I can tie it together. I say to myself that I'll sleep better, tonight anyway, knowing we have him caged. But tomorrow, they—whoever they are— can hire another gun. It occurred to me that Feona did the hiring, but not alone, and believe me, Feona is no housekeeper."

"Then what is she?"

"What do you think?" he asked Wainwright. "I saw her dead in the bathtub, and that doesn't tell me too much. But you interrogated her the first time, when the man in the tub was murdered. What was your impression of Feona Scott?"

"She was in command," Wainwright said. "You got the sense of what command means in the army, and it never leaves you. I would see a line officer killed, and the sergeant who should have taken over would turn into crud, and then some guy would step in and take command. It wasn't that she dumped on Eve Mackenzie; she just took over and apparently she always took over wherever she was. At least, that was my feeling."

"She was no housekeeper, right?"

"No, no way. She was a pro, Masao—but in what line I don't know."

"Do you think she was his mistress?" Masuto asked.

"Not in that sense. I mean not as a mistress. She was something else. Sex? That's something else. Sure, maybe they had sex."

Sergeant Cooper interrupted to tell them that he had finally located Dr. Baxter, having dinner at La Scala.

"He eats in fancy places. What do you want him for?"

"Will he come?" Masuto asked.

"When he finishes eating," Sergeant Cooper replied. "He wasn't very pleasant about being interrupted at dinner."

"*Pleasant* is a word he don't know," Wainwright said.

"Captain, what do I do about this guy the sergeant brought in?"

"We'll let you know."

"What about Sweeney?" Masuto asked.

"Be here in ten minutes."

"Let us know as soon as he arrives. I want his prints and I want them quickly."

Then he and Wainwright went to the room where the gunman sat under the observant eye of Officer Garcia. It was not an interrogation room. It would not have done for so civilized and quiet a place as Beverly Hills to have an interrogation room, but it served the same purpose, and the gunman sat backward on a wooden kitchen chair, his wrists still cuffed behind him.

"For Christ's sake," he begged them, "take them damn cuffs off. They're killing me. You the boss?" he demanded of Wainwright. "This goddamn Chinaman of yours, he broke my wrist and he broke my finger. Look at my pants—they're soaked with blood."

"You don't like pain, do you?" Masuto said. He went behind him and removed the handcuffs. Officer Garcia stood at the door.

"Outside," Wainwright said to Garcia. "Stay at the door."

"Can I take a leak?" the gunman begged them.

"I don't know," Wainwright said plaintively. "I swear to God I don't know what is happening to this country. Do you know who Norman Rockwell was, Masao? Or are you too young?"

"I remember the covers he used to do for the *Saturday Evening Post* when I was a kid."

"Well, look at this loathsome turd sitting there, this miserable and disgusting imitation of a human being. He could have stepped out of one of Norman Rockwell's paintings, with his pretty face and his blue eyes and his blond hair. If he isn't a faggot already, they'll turn him into one three days after he sets foot in San Quentin, but that won't last. After he's been gang-raped forty, fifty times, he goes to the gas chamber. After all, an easy way to die. Or do they keep them in solitary until the execution?"

"I don't know," Masuto said. "You can't be sure he'll be executed. Maybe we can't prove he killed Clint."

"You'll prove it. He's Masao Masuto," he said to the gunman. "You know what his record is? There has not been a murder in this city over the past ten years that he hasn't solved, not to mention attempted murder. You didn't take the money you were paid to kill a nobody. Your contract was for someone special—and that is why you have a ticket to the gas chamber."

"I didn't kill no guy named Clint! I don't know anybody named Clint!"

"Attempted murder," Masao said thoughtfully. "That's no problem. Two blasts from a sawed-off shotgun. We have the car, or what's left of it, the gun, and this poor misguided fool here. What would he get on the attempted murder, Captain? Fifteen to thirty?"

"They'd bugger him to death the first six months, but we're going to send him to the gas chamber."

"Well, if he cooperated—what's your name?"

"Hank Dobson."

"Your real name?"

"I told you. Look, I got a right to a lawyer. I got a right to a doctor."

"I'm sure you have," Wainwright agreed.

Officer Garcia opened the door a crack and said, "Sweeney's here."

"Come on in, Sweeney. Got your stuff?"

"All right here. I'll use this bench," Sweeney said.

"I want good prints," Wainwright said. "You make any fuss, mister, we break the other arm."

"I'm not making any fuss," he pleaded with Sweeney. "But my wrist is broken. It hurts like hell every time you touch my hand."

"You can make it hard on yourself or you can make it easy on yourself," Masuto said.

"I told you, I don't know nobody named Clint."

"Who hired you?"

"I don't know."

"You know something," Wainwright said. "If you had killed an L.A. cop and they had you like this, incognito so to speak, you'd never walk out of that door alive—"

"Pray none of this ever gets to the L.A. cops," Masuto said to himself.

"—but here in Beverly Hills," Wainwright went on, "well, it's a different picture. We can't use torture or force, but suppose you have to go two or three days with that broken wrist. Maybe you'd never use that hand again. Now the sergeant here, he wants to be kind to you. I don't know why. Maybe it's all this Oriental crap he's mixed up in."

"I'd like to help him," Masuto said. "A human being—"

"A turd!" Wainwright interrupted. "A shitheel!"

"Come on, come on, Captain. You're being too hard on him. He's human. If we can help him, we should."

"If he lets us."

"Got ten beautiful prints," Sweeney said.

"Put them on the wire for the F.B.I. Get everything they have."

"Help us help you," Masuto said to the gunman. "Who hired you?"

"I don't know. I told you I don't know. I wasn't lying."

"What you're saying makes no sense," Masuto said ingratiatingly. Wainwright allowed Masuto to take over now. "We know you're a pro. That shotgun thing tonight was absolutely the work of a pro. So when you say you don't know who hired you—well, it makes no sense at all."

"I don't."

"You know, you could do a lot of good for yourself. It's not that we don't care about you. We do. But our real interest is in the people who hired you. I'm not saying you're not in trouble; you are neck-deep in trouble, but wouldn't it be a nice thing for you if we could go to the district attorney or even to the judge and say, this fellow—what did you say your name was?"

He didn't slip. "Hank Dobson."

"Okay, we say to them, this fellow Hank Dobson, you know, without him we never would have made the bust, and we really busted somebody. That would help."

"Look, Sergeant, I keep a place in San Francisco. I don't mind telling you because I figure there's no bail anyway, and anyway I don't keep a place very long. People in the business know about my place, and you work by recommendation. Three days ago, I got a phone call—"

"Man or woman?"

"Man."

"Any accent?"

"Careful, correct talk. He was a foreigner, but that's just a guess. Asks me if I'm free and can take on a job. I say it depends. He tells me it's a Beverly Hills cop. I tell him that's thirty thousand dollars. A half hour later, a messenger comes with the money and your name."

"That's a sleazy story," Masuto said, "full of loose ends. I don't buy it. How did you know where to find me? How did you know I'd be up in

Malibu Canyon? How did you find out which was my car? Nobody followed me to the Mackenzie house. You were sitting there waiting. And where's the money?"

"Shit on all that," he said, and grinned and shook his head.

Wainwright went to the door and called for another cop named Sandy, and told the two of them to search Dobson, pile his possessions, and then stay with him. At the same time, a very short-tempered Dr. Baxter entered the room.

"I'm a medical examiner, not a doctor. Who's going to pay for this, that miserable chintzy city you work for? And why was I led to believe it was a corpse?"

"I can take care of that, Doc, if it's going to make you happy. This is the bag of human garbage murdered Oscar Clint. He'd be a lot prettier as a corpse."

"What is this?" Dobson shouted at Wainwright. "You going to leave me with these creeps?"

"He has a broken wrist, Doc."

"And a broken finger."

"Then why don't you take him to the hospital?"

"He likes it here." Wainwright drew Baxter out into the corridor. "We have a problem. He doesn't belong to us. He belongs to the L.A. cops. But we're pretty certain that he killed Clint by setting that bomb, and he tried to kill Masao here tonight."

"Did he?" Baxter asked, smiling evilly. "You don't have a scratch, Sergeant. He's a bungler."

"That's very amusing," Masuto said. "Nevertheless, we have a problem. The captain will have enough explaining to do downtown. We've had some run-ins in the past, and they don't exactly love me, so we have to put our best foot forward—"

"Did you break his wrist?" Baxter demanded.

"It was unavoidable."

"Patch him up nicely," Wainwright said. "The cops downtown will jump on anything, and what we don't need is any charge that we're torturing that miserable offal in there."

Baxter shook his head in disgust. "Cops," he said. "Cops."

"I can't figure him," Wainwright said as they went into his office. "All these years he worked for the city and I still can't figure him."

"He's a complex man," Masuto said.

In Wainwright's office, he telephoned Kati at his Uncle Toda's house, and she said to him, "We were expecting you, and then when you didn't come I called the police station. They said that someone had destroyed your car but you were all right."

"What idiot told you that?"

"I don't know, Masao, because I was too frightened even to ask his name, and all I could think of was how poor Oscar Clint had died in your car—"

"Please don't cry," he said to her. "I'm all right. I don't have a scratch on me. Please, Kati, don't cry."

"Will you come?" she begged him.

"If I can find a car—"

"Take one of the prowl cars," Wainwright said. "Bring it back in the morning and we'll find you a rental."

"In about an hour," Masuto said to Kati.

"Have you eaten?"

"I'm not hungry." In his state of tension and excitement, food was the last thing on his mind. "How are the children?"

She was crying again as she told him that the children were fine.

"You can't blame her," Wainwright said. "I never had anyone put a price on me. I don't know how I'd take it. But maybe since we got that blond turd inside, you can rest easy."

"Not until we find out who hired him and why."

"Then for God's sake, be careful."

"I'm always careful," Masuto said.

Sweeney came into the room with the F.B.I. response to the fingerprints. "They also sent the stuff on your question about the social security card." He handed two sheets of paper to Wainwright.

"Well, you were right about his name," Wainwright said to Masuto. "According to the F.B.I., his name is Albert Dexel, and he's got a reputation on several continents. They've never been able to hang it on him here at home, but they want him for murder in Paris and in Copenhagen, and they think he has some connection with the P.L.O. That's pretty good for something out of a *Saturday Evening Post* cover. And it also gives me a shoe-in with the L.A.P.D. We'll hand the collar over to them, and it's just classy enough for them to forget that you busted the creep on their turf. Now, this one—" He was reading the report on Feona Scott. "I'll be damned. Feona Scott was born in Baltimore, Maryland, in 1941. She died in a car crash in Dallas, Texas. So the good Feona's card was not only a forgery, it was a forgery based on an actual card. How the hell do they do that?"

"Either steal the original or have access to the records."

"Either way, the F.B.I. wants us to file a report on why we made the inquiry and on anyone using the card. Masao, what in hell are we dealing with?"

"I intend to find out."

"Well, try to stay alive until you do—if that's not too much to ask."

"Its not too much to ask." The captain handed him the two F.B.I reports, and Masuto glanced through them.

"What about blue-eyes in there?" Wainwright asked him. "You want to have a shot at him again?"

Masuto shrugged. "I don't know. I think that he was telling the truth —at least part of the truth. I don't think he knows who hired him. I think he may have had contact and taken directions from Feona, but that doesn't mean he knows any more about her than we do, which isn't very much. You can work him over, but it's been a long day for me. I'm tired. I want to see Kati and the kids and then sleep."

"Go ahead," Wainwright said magnanimously. "It's been three long, lousy days. The city doesn't pay for twelve- and fourteen-hour days. So take off and get some rest."

Masuto broke the speed limits, one of the privileges of being in a prowl car. Kati was waiting for him. Masuto was persuaded to eat a cheese omelet, and he and Kati sat at the kitchen table in the silent, sleeping house, whispering. A hot bath was waiting. And after that, Masuto lay in bed with his wife in his arms, forgetting a world he lived in but had never made.

22

The morning was lovely. There was a rumor in southern California that in the San Fernando Valley the months of July, August, and September were hot, smoggy, and unbearable, but all rumors are unreliable, and here was a morning at the end of August as cool as a mountaintop and as sweet as honey. The aroma of oranges lay over Uncle Toda's place like an olfactory blessing, and the air was full of glistening green hummingbirds, suspended over flowers in the heady joy of a hummingbird's existence. Masuto had never seen so many hummingbirds, and he had a feeling that they lived perpetually in the satori that he dreamed of achieving.

He was up with the sun, dressed and outside by six o'clock, as were Ana and Uraga, and with one of his children hanging on to each hand, he took a morning walk down to the irrigation canal and back, fending off the stream of questions the children directed at him, and thinking of a kinder day in the past, when children did not watch television news programs.

"But why should they want to kill you?" Ana pleaded. "You're good. You're the best daddy."

"No one wants to kill me, darling, believe me."

Uraga, taking a defensive and knowing stance, told his sister that it was a lot of hooey. "You think those reporters know what they're talking about? No, sir. They just think they do. Nobody's trying to kill Pop. They wouldn't dare. They couldn't."

Kati made pancakes, and Masuto found himself filling his stomach with a great mound of pancakes soaked with honey. His aunt and uncle had only tea and rice cakes for breakfast. Kati asked when they might go home. Uraga didn't want to go home, ever. Ana loved both places equally. The aunt and uncle smiled and begged them to stay; it was so wonderful having children and young people around.

"Tomorrow, I hope," Masuto said. "School starts next week."

"Will it be over tomorrow, truly?" Kati asked him.

"I hope so."

Driving back to Beverly Hills, he tried to work it out in his mind. It was full of imponderables, but his life was always threaded with imponderables. He would create a schematic of many-shaped pieces and hope that they would all fall into place. Sometimes they did; more often they didn't. Now he felt uneasy as a civilian driving a prowl car, and when he stopped for a light at Ventura Boulevard, an L.A. motorcycle cop pulled up alongside of him and stared suspiciously. Rather than submit to the motorcycle cop tailing him into Beverly Hills and then explaining that the sight of an Oriental in civilian clothes was suspicious, Masuto flashed his badge.

At the police station, Beckman was waiting for him in full uniform, his oversized bulk bulging at the seams, the brass buttons ready to pop.

"I'll just go inside and change," Masuto said. "We'll use your car today, if you don't mind."

"Everyone says it's the end of a very nice Dodge. They got you pegged as a car destroyer. But I'm insured."

"Good. We won't worry about it."

"As long as we're not inside it when it goes."

Masuto grinned and went into the station.

"You put me to shame," Beckman said when Masuto reappeared in full uniform. "You haven't gained an ounce."

"Japanese food. It's not fattening. Now, what about tonight, Sy? Did you explain to your wife?"

"I tried. What a ball my life would be if her suspicions were only true. That's what burns me up, not that she's suspicious, but that I don't measure up."

"That's only because you don't have the time," Masuto consoled him. "Not because you're unattractive. You're a hard-working cop."

"No talent," Beckman muttered.

At the Church of Our Lady, the uniformed cops were grouped outside under the direction of one Lieutenant Chester. He instructed Masuto and Beckman to join the four pallbearers already selected. "I think it's only proper, Sergeant. Don't you?"

Masuto nodded.

"You'll be sitting at the front of the church. The rear rows are reserved for the honor guard. When the honor guard leaves, we'll form two rows. Hats off in a civilian salute. No guns or anything like that."

"Out of the church and into the funeral car? Is that it?" one of the pallbearers asked.

"That's right."

"What about the cemetery?"

"We have a limo for cops. Four men who were close to Clint are signed for it. We can take two more."

Two hands went up. Masuto felt a twinge of guilt, but it would have been a pretense if he had volunteered. He had never been friendly with Clint. While they were standing there, Clint's wife and children went into the church. She looked strangely at Masuto. Well, that was only to be expected. In a way, as unreasonable as it was, she had to hold him at least partly responsible for her husband's death.

In the church, Masuto sat uncomfortably, feeling eyes turned toward him, feeling strange in his uniform. In spite of the fact that Buddhism excluded no other faith, Masuto never felt at ease in a church, and in this case, every word of the priest's remarks appeared to seek him out. Beckman's whisper into his ear was welcome.

"Who do you think is sitting seven, eight rows behind us?"

"I'm not turning around," Masuto muttered.

"I'll fill you in. Mark Geffner and Jo Hardin, namely Eve Mackenzie's sister."

Masuto had the next twenty minutes to brood about that bit of information—until with the other pallbearers, he slid the coffin into the hearse. Then he even managed to say a few necessary words to Mrs. Clint, who was no doubt saying to herself, why not him instead of my husband? But it was managed, and then the funeral cortege pulled away, and Masuto was left there vowing that he would not go through this again, not if it meant resigning from the force. And then he turned around and saw Geffner and Jo Hardin talking to Beckman.

Masuto joined them. Geffner shook hands with him enthusiastically and remarked that he looked very good in uniform, and then introduced him to Jo Hardin, a tall, remarkably beautiful woman for her age, which was fifty-one.

"What we would like," Geffner said, "is to talk to both of you, and if you're free for lunch, that would be a very good time, since Jo has to get back to Montecito this afternoon."

"Nothing would please me more," Masuto agreed.

"I got to get out of this uniform," Beckman said. "I'm choking, and if I bend over too far, everything goes."

"We'll change and meet you at Mario's at twelve-thirty. You know the place?" he asked Geffner.

"On Olympic?"

"The food's edible and the prices are within a cop's budget. You know we got to go dutch."

"Wouldn't have it any other way."

Geffner and Jo Hardin were already there and waiting when Masuto and Beckman arrived. They ordered their food and then made some conversation about the funeral, Geffner sympathizing with Masuto's discomfort.

"I would have crawled out of it," Geffner said. "She has to resent you —her husband killed in your car with a bomb intended for you. It must have been a very rough morning."

"Very rough, but no use to talk about it. It's done. When a man's life is taken, nothing puts it back."

"No, of course not. But that isn't what we want to talk to you about, Sergeant. Let me first put the record straight about Jo and myself. This is a woman I love very much, and we'll be married in about a month from now. I think I fell in love with Jo the first time I saw her, which was shortly after Mackenzie's death—or rather after the death of the man in the tub. After her sister's death followed so soon by the death of Feona Scott, Jo felt that we must talk."

"On the wedding," Masuto said, "congratulations. On your desire to talk to us, well, I'm grateful. We need every bit of help we can get."

"First of all," Jo Hardin said, "you know that my sister was an alcoholic?"

Masuto nodded.

"A most peculiar kind of alcoholic. You know there are alcoholics that pass out, that become disgustingly drunk—others who are unable to talk, others who become sick and nasty. My sister was none of those. Drunk, she assumed great dignity, and the drunker she got, the greater the dignity. She spoke slowly with great calm, and she could fool most people. But she was still sodden drunk, her judgment, her mind—well, that was her condition. I loved her very much. I don't know what drove her to destroy herself, but she killed herself as surely as if she had put a gun to her head. When her car went over the cliff side, it may or may not have been deliberate, but if it hadn't happened then, it would have happened sooner or later. When Robert was around, he almost never permitted her to drive."

"We heard that he beat her," Masuto said, "that she hated him."

"That's nonsense. Beat her! Indeed! That's the stuff that those people at Fenwick put out when they talked her into going on trial. They offered her money, the house—all sorts of things. Robert never beat her. He had such patience—he must have loved her very much, and you would understand that if you knew my sister. Drunk or not, she was a beautiful and charming woman."

"I'll buy that," Beckman said.

"Did she know why they wanted to put her on trial?" Masuto asked. "That's at the crux of this matter, and I can't make head or tail out of it. I have theories—"

"So have I," Geffner cut in. "Let's hear yours."

"There's really only one explanation that holds water," Masuto said. "Everything else I've thought of breaks down."

"Go on," Geffner said eagerly.

"Well, there's no question in my mind that Feona Scott killed the man in the tub, not alone, but I have the feeling that she conked him over the head. So I have to draw the conclusion that they worked out the charade with Eve Mackenzie to cover up Feona's guilt."

"You mean once Simpkins closed the book on her, threw the case out of court, it was over."

"Something changed," Masuto said. "Your sister's death, the empty coffin. Let's look at it this way: there are a number of people in Washington who don't want Feona prosecuted for murder. Why? If she's one of their agents, if she's C.I.A., then they surely would try to avoid the scandal and smell of murder. But—" he turned to Jo Hardin—"what do you think? Do you think Feona Scott was a C.I.A. agent?"

"I don't know—why? Why would the C.I.A. plant an agent in my sister's home?"

"It was also Mackenzie's home."

"Yes—but—"

"How long ago did Feona come to work at the Mackenzies'?"

"About four years ago."

"Do you know how they hired her, how they found her?"

"No, I'm afraid not," Jo said.

"Tell me something else, Miss Hardin. Your brother-in-law, Robert Mackenzie—did he have a heavy Scottish accent?"

"Rather heavy—yes."

"Did he ever tell you where he was born and educated?"

"Oh, yes, Edinburgh. But, you know, whatever you're thinking of Robert—well, all I can say is that he was endlessly tender and patient with Eve. When Eve heard that he would never come back—"

"What!"

"You never mentioned that to me," Geffner said.

"Didn't I? But I was sworn to silence about so many things, and it's only a few days since Eve died. You see, Eve knew immediately that the man in the tub was not Robert. Not only were certain scars that Robert had missing, but a woman knows. Of course, it must have been Robert's twin brother. Well, they told her that Robert had left for Canada before the murder. Eve did not drive up to my house. Robert brought her to my house and left the car there. I drove him to the airport, and then the following morning Eve insisted on returning to Beverly Hills. But Robert was actually in an airplane on his way to Canada when the murder took place. So neither he nor Eve could have done it."

"No, of course not," Masuto agreed, "but you mentioned something about Eve finding out that her husband would not come back."

"Yes. You see, at the beginning, when they talked Eve into that ridiculous trial, they insinuated that when it was over, Robert would come back and they could resume their life in Beverly Hills. Poor Eve was out on bail, staying with me at that moment and talking about her life with Robert when he returned and what she would do, and possibly joining Alcoholics Anonymous and even adopting a child, and most of it was the bottle talking, except her statement that Robert would return. I asked her who told her that, and she said her lawyer, Mr. Cassell. Well, you can imagine that I did not tell her how ridiculous it was. It would have been too much for her to bear. But a few days later, I was in Beverly Hills and I went to Mr. Cassell's office and asked him how he dared to delude my poor sister in this manner. How could Robert ever return? They were moving heaven and earth for the world to believe him dead. How could he return?" she demanded of Masuto.

"He couldn't. But how did Mr. Cassell persuade you to remain silent?"

"For Eve's good, for Eve's benefit, just be patient, no, it doesn't mean she'll never see her husband again, just give us time to straighten this out and everything will fall into place, and then Eve can join her husband. But I don't think they ever intended Eve to join Robert again. They intimated that a drunk could not be dealt with. Poor Eve—to be so badly used, and all her beauty and talent just wasted—" She was close to tears.

"Miss Hardin," Masuto said gently, "during those years when your sister and Robert Mackenzie were together, you would see them?"

"Of course."

"Fairly often? Once a week? Once a month?"

"No—Christmas, Easter, once or twice a year they'd invite me to go sailing with them. Robert was a good sailor. He had a twenty-seven-foot sloop—"

"You say he had it. Did he sell it?"

"I don't know. It never entered my mind."

"And where did he berth it?"

"At Oxnard, which was convenient for me, halfway between here and Santa Barbara."

The men exchanged glances. Geffner was about to speak when Masuto shook his head slightly, and Geffner swallowed his words.

"I was wondering," Masuto said, "whether in the time you knew Robert Mackenzie—whether during that time any questions arose in your mind?"

Geffner and Beckman had both of them put away large plates of pasta. Masuto had nibbled at a sandwich. The salad in front of Jo Hardin remained untouched.

"Questions?"

"About Robert Mackenzie."

"Well, he was a rather depressed personality. But that is not unusual among the Scots, is it?"

"I don't know. Did you ever doubt that he was Scottish?"

She thought about it. "No—no, not really. I remember on New Year's Eve, he sang 'Auld Lang Syne' with a wonderful Scottish accent, and not just the first verse but the whole song. It was wonderful." She wiped her eyes. "I seem to cry at everything today. It's the funeral, I think, so soon after poor Eve's cremation. And once in a while, he'd read to us from Robert Burns. I never knew how Burns should sound or what it meant until I heard Robert read it. You know, there's a sound in Scots that is almost impossible for Americans to make—the sound *och*. You see, I can't really make it either, and I remember one night he was trying to teach us how to do it—it was such fun."

"Then there's no doubt in your mind, Miss Hardin, that Robert Mackenzie is a valid Scot?"

"Oh, no—no. I have sat and listened to him narrate the history of the Mackenzies, and they were such great people. Robert was descended from the famous Scottish lawyer, Sir George Mackenzie, who was born in Dundee in 1636. You see, I remember the date, Robert spoke of him so often, and of Sir George's defense of the Marquis of Argyll, who was tried for high treason. You see, Robert's branch of the family became very poor and stayed poor, so while many other Mackenzies are in *Who's Who*, Robert still had that as his goal, as if to vindicate the

Mackenzie name in what he felt was the stain placed upon his father and grandfather."

Listening to her, Masuto had the impression that she was not a little enraptured with her sister's husband—perhaps all unknown to herself.

"Yet he wasn't in *Who's Who,* was he?"

"I'm afraid not, Sergeant Masuto."

"Yet I've heard him described as one of the most brilliant engineers in America."

"By whom?" Geffner wondered.

"Oh? Let me see." He turned to Beckman. "What about it, Sy?"

"Did you tell me that, Masao?"

"If you have any doubts about Robert's brilliance, you can set them at rest. He perfected the heat-seeking automatic pilot that guides a missile to its target."

"Yet he isn't in *Who's Who,*" Masuto said.

Geffner said, "I'm afraid you're wrong, darling. I was reading about that particular weapon. I don't think it was devised by a Robert Mackenzie."

"I'm not wrong," she said with irritation. "Eve told me."

"Well, I could be wrong," Geffner said gently. "I think we've told Sergeant Masuto and Detective Beckman all that we know that might be helpful." And to Masuto, "Are you sure we can't pick up your check? Heaven knows, it's small enough."

"Small enough for us to pay it," Masuto insisted.

Outside, and in Beckman's car, Masuto said to Beckman, "Come on, I want your reaction—quick and off the top of your head."

"I think she had a case on her sister's husband. I hope Mark can live with it. He's a nice guy."

"He'll live with it. What about Mackenzie?"

"He's very good, isn't he? Very big with Scottish patriotism or culture or whatever you'd call it. You ever heard of this Sir George Mackenzie?"

"I'm not up on Scottish history, but I'm sure that if we look him up, we'll find him there, just where Robert says he's supposed to be."

"You know, Masao, we never had a case like this one, where everything is stood on its head, and we never had a case where not one damn bit of it made any sense."

"Oh, I think it's beginning to make a little sense."

"For you, maybe."

"No, it's when people do things contrary to law and decency that it becomes turgid and beyond understanding. Understanding is condi-

tioned by some rules of humanity. When you drop all the rules, understanding revolts. So much for that. Now, let's go back to the station
house where I can yell my head off at Sweeney."

"Because he hasn't come up with Feona Scott's prints?"

"Precisely."

"Blame me. I should have told you. Shelly Langer at Records called
me in early this morning and told me that the F.B.I. showed nothing for
our Feona. I told her to wire every source, including Scotland Yard. She
should have something when we get back."

But back at the station house, Shelly Langer had only an inviting
smile. As for Feona Scott, "This lady never existed," Miss Langer said.

"She existed. She was alive and now she's dead."

"But no fingerprints anywhere, Sergeant. Either she was careful, or
she was a farm gal who lived a life of great purity and never set foot out
of Kansas."

"It gets curiouser and curiouser," said Masuto, who read *Alice in
Wonderland* to his children.

23

"It's half past two," Beckman said. "Would you mind giving me an agenda for the rest of today? Didn't you mention that you told Kati she could come home with the kids tomorrow?"

"I said she might, and I shouldn't have said that. Where did Geffner and his new lady say they were going?"

"To Eve's house, I think. Geffner got her the key."

"Yes, of course. Eve died intestate, and with Mackenzie legally dead, the whole thing goes to Jo."

"But Mackenzie isn't dead."

"Oh, no," Masuto said. "Mackenzie is dead. The State of California declared him a murder victim and tried Eve for his murder."

"Technicality."

"Sy, we live in a very technical world. Let's stop over at Lexington Road. One very important question I never asked Jo Hardin."

Both Geffner and Miss Hardin were surprised to see the two policemen, and Geffner said to Masuto, "It shakes you, because the guilt in this thing is so tenuous, so amorphous, that you begin to feel a part of it."

"No, we have no suspicions, please believe me. Only I forgot to ask Miss Hardin what were the relations between Eve Mackenzie and Feona Scott."

"Eve hated her."

"Ah, so!" Masuto shook his head with annoyance. "All that time at lunch, I never asked you the important question. Of course, you intrigued me with your description of Robert Mackenzie, but afterward, thinking about it, I remembered that you had called him depressed. But your description was not of a depressed man—no, indeed. You described an ebullient man."

She thought about it for a while. "Yes, I suppose I did."

"Now, please, think about this, Miss Hardin. Depression is an illness that affects a man's entire personality. Unhappiness is simply a condition of being human. A person could be deeply unhappy without having a pathological case of depression. So please tell me, were there long periods when Robert Mackenzie was not depressed?"

Again, she thought about it. "Yes, I believe so."

"Ah. Before Feona Scott arrived?"

"Yes, now that you mention it."

"Do you think," Masuto asked slowly, "that he was having an affair with Feona Scott?"

On this, she didn't hesitate. "Good heavens, no!"

"Why so violent?"

"Because he detested her."

"But kept her on and paid her wages. You told me before that you saw your sister only occasionally. How can you be so certain about the relationships in their household?"

"Come on, Masuto," Geffner protested, "there's no reason to interrogate Jo in this manner. She came forward to volunteer the information."

"I am not interrogating her. I am investigating a case in which three people have already been murdered, and you and I survive only by virtue of luck and your superior driving. I have to ask questions, Mr. Geffner. You know that as well as I do."

"Mark, please let me answer. You see, Sergeant, you can see people only once in a while yet be very close to them, and I was close to my sister and Robert. I once asked him why he hired Feona Scott, and he said something about how hard it was to find someone willing to take care of an alcoholic. That happens to be true, and I suppose that's the reason why he kept her on. But he did not sleep with her and he did not like her."

"Did he ever say what part of Scotland she came from? She was born in Scotland?"

"I think he once mentioned the slums of Glasgow."

Masuto and Beckman were back in the car, driving out on Sunset Boulevard toward the Pacific, when Masuto said, "Twins from Edinburgh who never existed and a maiden fair from Glasgow. Trouble is, she drew a better name than Mackenzie. I've never looked at a Glasgow telephone book, but I presume there are more Scotts there than one could shake a stick at and even a few Feonas."

"And now," Beckman said, "since you suggested that we drive west on Sunset, I presume we're returning to the Fenwick Works. I see it on television all the time, the stupid cops walking into the bad guys' trap. Suppose they put us in a vat or something and dissolve us with some fancy acid."

"I think they'll be very polite, and anyway, it's a nice day for a ride along the Pacific."

It was such a day. There was no smog, and the sky over the ocean was alive with small cumulus clouds, a rare thing for this time of the year. At the gate to Fenwick, Masuto showed his badge, and after a few words on the phone the guard waved him in. The same efficiency at the door of the main building, after which they were told that Mr. Soames would be delighted to talk with Sergeant Masuto and Detective Beckman. They had to wait ten minutes, but during that time they were served coffee by a tall, pretty, young woman.

In his office, Soames greeted them pleasantly and told them to sit down. "What can I do for you gentlemen?"

"I would like to ask you some questions," Masuto said. "Of course, you have the right not to answer and you also have the right to tell us to leave. But I'm sure you're aware of that."

"Indeed I am."

"All right. Have you ever heard the name Albert Dexel?"

"No."

"Why did you try to detain me the other day?"

"It was a clumsy and stupid effort, for which I apologize with all my heart. For an American businessman to resort to any such thing is utterly deplorable. But I had two people coming up from Washington, and they were most eager to talk to you, and they begged me to keep you here even if I had to handcuff you to do it."

"Then why didn't they come to the Beverly Hills police headquarters and talk to me there?"

"After our discussion, they changed their minds."

"Yes, of course. Do you know where Robert Mackenzie is?"

"No, I don't. But I presume he's still in Canada."

"No, he isn't—or at least he was not in Canada yesterday. Yesterday he killed Feona Scott."

"Oh? I saw no such accusation in this morning's paper. Or is this another secret of the Beverly Hills police?"

"Isn't it time we stopped playing games, Mr. Soames. This is not an entertainment we're discussing. It's murder, and Robert Mackenzie is guilty of that murder. You know it and I know it, and we both know why he shot Feona Scott. Let him give up and be tried—"

"No!"

"Scott killed his twin brother. You have the best lawyers in California. You can certainly get a mitigated sentence."

"Sergeant Masuto," Soames said, "I am trying to be very patient with you. You are a fine and honest policeman, and I respect anyone who does a good job of work. I am not trying to hoodwink you or to tamper with the law. But you function on a certain level, and there are other levels in this great nation of ours. The Mackenzie case is closed, and for all purposes, legal and otherwise, Robert Mackenzie has ceased to exist. This is not from me, but from people far more powerful and important in the scheme of things."

"Are there levels," Masuto wondered, "where murder is not murder?"

"Sergeant, we live in a different world than what existed when we were children. Murder has become a way of international relationship. Consider Iran, the P.L.O., Libya, Bulgaria—murder is simply a word, and in defense of national policy and national security, it is condoned."

Masuto felt a shiver run up his spine. What does one say? What is good and what is bad? "I am a policeman who works in Beverly Hills," Masuto said quietly. "When a murder is committed in a house in Beverly Hills, I must find the perpetrator."

"That's simply rigid and unthinking."

"Perhaps."

"You will not find Mr. Mackenzie. Give it up."

"It used to be simpler to be a cop," Beckman said once they were outside.

"You can say that again. Where now?"

"Oxnard?"

"Why not? A boat is a good place to hide. He could sail out to one of those uninhabited islands off the Santa Barbara channel and really go to earth."

"You think so?"

"No, but we're partway there, so why not? You see, Sy, the good folk who have been trying to kill me are now after Mackenzie. It has to play that way. He killed Scott, and now he must disappear. Whatever the game is, he's played it for a long time. At first he was a stranger, a blank face, but bit by bit he comes into focus. He must have loved Eve Mackenzie; that's the romantic part of him; but it was a passion that survived her alcoholism, and if you ever dealt with an alcoholic, you know what that means."

"I can see what you're getting at," Beckman said. "He was her husband. Your wife dies—"

"Yes, he must have come back on that basis. Consider that he's been waiting for an opportunity to revenge himself on Feona. He takes it, but where does he go to ground—hotels? No, too dangerous. No friend could be trusted."

"Jo Hardin."

"I think so. The question is, did Geffner know?"

"Come on, Masao—that's his life, his career."

"I hope he didn't know."

They drove on to Oxnard, Masuto still trying to think his way out of the maze of the past four days. But the short drive to the Oxnard marina left no time for mental escape, and the white boats, lying so still in the golden sunlight, vitiated any concept of the forces of evil. The marina manager, after he had looked at their credentials, shook his head and said, "Funny, that boat's been here for months, and no one gave a damn about it. You're the third one to come asking about it today."

"Two other people asking about the Mackenzie boat?"

"That's right."

"Cops. Officers of any kind?"

"Nope."

"Which boat is it?" Beckman asked.

"Slip thirty-two."

"Which way?"

"I'll take you over there," he said with a snicker. They followed him out onto a long wooden deck to a slip that was numbered 32.

"I don't see the boat," Beckman said.

"You're looking the wrong way. Down there." He pointed into the water, and there beneath them, sitting in twenty feet of water, was a beautiful sloop.

"Last night," the marina manager said, "someone opened the cocks. Down she went."

"Anyone in there?"

"No, we sent a diver down. No one in it." He stepped aside to give them a clear view, and then he said, "There's the guy looked at it before."

He stood at the end of the pier, a tall, broad-shouldered, well-dressed man, blondish hair, steel-rimmed glasses. Both Masuto and Beckman plunged into action, racing down the pier, Beckman, for all his size and weight, a trifle faster than Masuto. When the man at the end of the pier saw them coming, he sprinted across the marina and across the road, dodging the cars like an open-field runner, and then up a slight bluff onto a field of dry, parched grass. Beckman gained on him as he was trying to scramble up the bluff, Beckman taking it by sheer momentum, and then, as he started across the field, Beckman tackled him above the knees, bringing him down with a mighty thud. As Masuto joined them, Beckman had gotten up and the man he tackled had rolled over and was trying to sit up.

"You big, dumb ape," the man on the ground said. "You've gone and broken my glasses and maybe busted a couple of ribs too."

"Who the hell are you calling an ape, mister? Just get the hell up out of there and identify yourself."

"Easy, Sy," Masuto whispered. "I think he's some kind of cop."

"You're damn right I am," the tackled man said, handing his identification to Masuto.

"God save us, he's a G-man, name of Peter Thatcher. Well, Peter," he said, handing the wallet back, "why did you run? Having done no wrong, which I trust was the case, why did you run?"

"Because, Masuto, having been told to avoid a smartass Jap cop under all circumstances, I tried to obey orders."

"That's very praiseworthy, but out here in California, and in other places too, I expect, the language you used is considered insulting and degrading. I would appreciate an apology and some confession of ignorance."

"Otherwise," Beckman said, "well, who is to say how hard you fell when I tackled you. A few more broken ribs can be explained."

"Come on, come on," Thatcher said. "I've been knocked over and maybe broke a rib and lost my glasses, so a little anger can be excused. Sure, I'm sorry. We're on the same side."

"Maybe."

"You guys just looking for Mackenzie, or do you know where he is?"

"Why did they tell you to steer clear of me?"

"I don't know."

"Does your bunch ever talk to the C.I.A.?" Beckman wondered.

"Can you drive?" Masuto asked him.

"I guess you don't know where Mackenzie is," Thatcher said. "If you did, you wouldn't be down here looking at his boat."

"Send an optician's voucher to our office, and they'll refund whatever the new glasses cost. Can you drive?"

"I always keep a spare pair in my car. Part of the burden of wearing glasses. But a word of advice, Masuto. They told me about an Oriental cop and that I should keep an eye peeled for him. Someone else might have opened up on you."

"That's part of the burden of being a Jap—as you put it," Masuto said. "But tonight I'm going to shed my burden. I'll be at home, in what I call my meditation room, meditating. It's a way of getting rid of some of what the world does to you."

"Oh, yes. You're a Zen Buddhist, as I recall." He offered his hand. "No hard feelings anyway."

They shook hands, and Thatcher strode off. Beckman stared at Masuto thoughtfully.

"Well?"

"That's what you'll be doing tonight, sitting there in your little meditation room, meditating?"

"Yes."

"I thought we were working together tonight. Did I have to talk my wife out of believing that I would be shacked up with some lady of small virtue and large boobs tonight—or was that just an exercise in persuasion?"

"You'll watch me."

"Yes, of course," Beckman mumbled. "That's as reasonable as everything else in this case. Sure. I'll enjoy watching you. Anyway, I think Thatcher took it all pretty well. I hit him like a ton of bricks."

When they were in the car, driving south on the Pacific Coast Highway, Masuto said to Beckman, "Stop at Alice's Restaurant. I want to use the phone there."

At the restaurant, Masuto put through a call to Los Angeles headquarters of the Federal Bureau of Investigation. Switched to Personnel, he said, "This is Detective Sergeant Masao Masuto of the Beverly Hills police force. I'm not there now, but here's my badge number, and I'll wait while you call them and verify. But make it quick. I'm in a phone booth, calling long distance." The lady at the other end said she'd take his number and call back. Beckman came in to see what was happening. Then the pay phone rang, and the lady from the Justice Department asked what she could do for Sergeant Masuto.

"I want to know whether there is a Peter Thatcher here in Los Angeles or in any other part of the service."

The computer was quicker than such mundane tasks as personal phone calls. The lady at the other end of the wire assured Masuto that no one named Peter Thatcher worked for the Justice Department, in the Bureau or anywhere else.

24

Wearing his saffron-colored terry-cloth robe and Japanese thong sandals, Masuto entered the living room, where Beckman sat eating peanuts and poring over an album of the pictures the Masutos had taken in Japan. Somewhat abashed, Masuto explained that the color of the robe had nothing to do with the quality of his meditation. "It's true the saffron color is favored by some orders of Buddhist priests, but it means nothing. It's a little conceit of mine. Some people who meditate burn incense. I don't—it makes me feel that I'm choking."

"You're sure about this—this meditation thing?"

"Well, yes, Sy—as sure as I can be about anything in this curious business. They've been here. They were careful, but not careful enough. They moved certain things and replaced them a bit off. Oh, they were here. They know all about me, but of meditation in any real sense, I'm sure they know nothing at all. Such people simply cannot comprehend what meditation is, and they will regard it as some sort of religious devotion that I must perform."

"I'm not sure that I know any more than they do."

"That's only because there's so very little to know. Meditation is a very simple matter, but this is not an age where simple matters are understood. Now, let's examine the battlefield." He turned down all the lamps except one. "I haven't thrown the bolt on the front door, so they will be able to slip-card it. They will come through that little vestibule and into the living room. There, through the living room to the sun porch. I call it my meditation room. Please." He motioned to Beckman to follow him, and then opened the glass doors to the sun porch. "We'll leave these wide open so that from the front door they will be able to see me sitting here and meditating."

For all the years he had known Masuto and worked with him, Beckman had never seen this small room before. It was about eight feet deep and ten feet wide, a porch with windows, built onto the back of the Culver City bungalow. Masuto had put grass blinds over the windows, grass-colored paper on the walls, and yellow vinyl on the floor. The room was completely bare, unfurnished except for a black mat and a black pillow.

Beckman shook his head. "Mostly I go along with you, Masao. But this—well, I just don't know why."

"Let me try to explain the way I see it—no, *feel* it is better, because I have only a sense of what may happen. Remember, nothing may happen. We may wait all night—and then nothing. But if they come—"

"Who?"

"You keep asking me, Sy. I don't know. Tonight we may find out, and I have to find out. I can't live like this. I find fear deplorable, and I have been constantly afraid. I don't enjoy being afraid."

"All right. You dropped the word with Thatcher—"

"Maybe. We look at it differently. From our point of view, they are watching the house. This is terribly important to them. Think of what ends they have gone to, removing the body, hiring Albert Dexel, and Thatcher—and who knows how many others. Apparently, money is no object."

"Damn it, who are they and what do they want?"

"This we find out tonight. Now, come with me." He led Beckman into Ana's bedroom, all pink and white. "You leave here by the front door, Sy, circle about ten blocks, and come in on the street behind us. The couple in that house—" he pointed through the window "—both work the night shift down at the airport. Go to the end of their driveway, and there's my hedge. Work your way through it and you're right there in the backyard. Your eyes will be used to the dark. I'll kill the light in this room, but you'll see me here. The window will be open, and you'll crawl through. We'll just hope that no one sees you, but they must be convinced that I am alone in the house."

Beckman sighed and nodded and left the house by the front door. Exactly seven minutes later, Masuto helped him crawl through Ana's window.

"You're right," he admitted. "They're in a car down the street."

"Yes, I imagined so. Now, over here, this French door leads from Ana's room onto the sun porch. I always keep it closed and the grass shade drawn, but as you can see, with the lights out here and the lamp on on the sun porch, you have a good view of the whole porch. I don't mind the children watching me meditate. I hope they're inclined to imitate me, but mostly I meditate before they awaken or after they sleep."

"I still don't understand why the meditation."

"All right, let me try to explain. They know I have a reputation for karate, but I don't want a contest. I don't want them coming in with guns. I sit in the lotus position, and a simple inquiry will tell them that in such a position, I am immobilized. I cannot leap to my feet. I am more or less defenseless. I want it that way. Even if they come to kill me, I want them to feel free to talk."

"That's great. Even if they come to kill you. That's great. That's absolutely brilliant. I hate to say this, Masao, but you sound like the number one shmuck of southern California."

"I suppose so."

"There's got to be another way to do this."

"No." His voice hardened. "We'll do it this way."

"What is with you? Can't I make a suggestion?"

"I'm putting my life in your hands," Masuto said. "We're too long good friends for you to get angry now. If at a point they try to kill me— well, it's up to you."

"Great. I need that."

"I trust you, Sy."

"Sure, I can see myself explaining to Kati why you're dead. Explaining it to Wainwright, thank God, will not be necessary. I'll be fired first."

"We'll both stay alive. And, Sy—"

"Yeah?"

"Don't interfere. Don't stop it. Don't breathe—unless it means my life or someone else's life. You can hear everything through this door. So take your position, and then we wait."

Sitting on a chair in the darkness behind the French door, Beckman watched Masuto remove his shoes and then compose himself in the lotus position on the small round cushion which he had placed on the black mat. He placed his hands together on his lap, one on top of the other, thumbs touching. His lids drooped as he stared at the floor in front of him and he became motionless, with only the rise and fall of his breath to say that there was life in the saffron-robed figure. It had been a long and difficult day, and in Ana's dark room, Beckman struggled to remain awake. He had drawn a chair up to the door, and he sat there, his big forty-five caliber automatic pistol in his hand, staring at the motionless figure of Masuto.

They must have decided to wait half an hour after Beckman had pretended to leave. The little house was hardly soundproof, and the noise of the door opening brought Beckman back from his half-doze, awake now and intent.

The man who entered the house and walked across the living room to face Masuto was about five feet nine inches, a tight body, a lined, severe face, intelligent blue eyes, and thin sandy hair. He was about forty-five years old. As Masuto looked up at him, he held out a hand, palm down, and said, "No, please don't rise Mr. Masuto. I prefer you in this position, and I have heard too much about the lethal power of your hands to want them on my level. Indeed, if you insist on rising, I will have to draw my gun, and I much prefer a conversation that is not at the point of a pistol."

"I have no intention of rising," Masuto assured him. "It is you who interrupt my meditation."

"For which I apologize." His English was excellent, but with a slight accent which Masuto guessed was Russian. "Let me introduce myself. My name is Alexander Brekov, and I am legal counsel to our ambassador in Washington. But that is simply a mutually understood subterfuge. I am actually a part of the K.G.B., and I tell you this without hesitation because it is well known to your F.B.I. and also to your C.I.A."

"Or possibly because you intend to kill me before you leave?" Masuto wondered.

"You are an interesting adversary, Mr. Masuto. Feona decided that you had to be destroyed. She was foolish, and the foolish die. I decided that you're a reasonable man. Zen Buddhists are reasonable men. I see no reason why you should be different."

"I like to think of myself as a reasonable man. Tell me, Mr. Brekov. Who was Feona Scott?"

"K.G.B." He half smiled. "You Americans love those three letters. She was a Russian agent." He shrugged. "Not the best. Let me explain. The man you know as Robert Mackenzie is a Soviet agent whose real name is Andre Rostikoff. Years of effort—very expensive effort—went into his training, from age fourteen. I can't tell you what it takes to take a Russian and turn him into a Scot—his memory of history and family, his language, his manner, his walk, his reactions—so that he becomes even more Scottish than a man born in Scotland. And do you know how Mr. Mackenzie, né Rostikoff, repaid the Soviet people? By becoming a double agent. We were not sure of this at first, but certain things in his reports aroused our suspicions, and Feona, whose real name was Sonia Dukovsky, was sent to join him and to find out what was going on. This she did. She obtained the proof that he was indeed working with the C.I.A., and that through his efforts, two of our agents were uncovered."

"And then, unexpectedly," Masuto said, "his twin brother appeared."

"Yes—I suppose that was obvious to you. His twin brother was one of those who attack us because we do not see civil liberties in the Western manner. He was a poet of sorts, a dissenter, and finally he was given the right to emigrate. Now, how he tracked down his brother out here in California, I don't know. Possibly there had been some communication; I suspect so. In any case, he showed up at the Mackenzie house at an unfortunate moment, with both Robert and his drunken wife away. I'm sure you know what happened. Feona lost her head and killed him, and then she phoned me, and I sent the man you know as Thatcher over there. His name is Gregory Roboff, and he's not very smart. By the way, he is sitting in the car across the street, and while he is not bright, he is an excellent shot. Just a remark. He allowed Feona to talk him into that crazy business of putting poor Ivan Rostikoff into the bathtub, because she read it in that drunken woman's notebook. Well, that is why Robert Mackenzie shot her. He is a sentimentalist. He avenged his brother's death." Now Brekov took out a package of Turkish cigarettes. "May I smoke?"

No one had ever smoked in his meditation room.

"There is an ashtray in the next room. You may bring it in here if you wish. You say Feona Scott desired me dead. Why? I did her no harm."

"She knew your reputation. She was sure you would find out too much too quickly."

"And you are here tonight to complete her unfinished business?"

"Oh, no. No, indeed. I am here to strike a bargain, to make a deal, as you people say, to create a mutually advantageous situation. I am sure you know what I want."

"Robert Mackenzie."

"Exactly. We are quite certain that you know where he is. I want you to tell me where he is." He reached into his jacket pocket and took out a packet of currency. "Here I have fifty hundred-dollar bills. I have four such packets, twenty thousand dollars. That is a great deal of money for a policeman, wouldn't you agree?"

"Yes, a great deal of money."

"And what am I asking, Mr. Masuto? The man is a traitor and a murderer. He has betrayed those who nurtured him and loved him. What call has he upon you?"

"I have never had to think that through," Masuto said, "because I don't know where he is."

"Come, come. Of course you do."

"Considering that I do know, Mr. Brekov, why should I take sides in your quarrel with him? I sit here doing a very simple thing, bringing harm to no one, sitting with my legs crossed and meditating in the manner of my ancestors. My master in downtown Los Angeles is an old Roshi. Would he be permitted to teach me in your country? Is there a Zendo anywhere in your country?"

"That is not the point. What is this country you are being loyal to? The only country that ever used the atom bomb—and used it to wipe out two Japanese cities—men, women, and children. This is the country you are being loyal to?"

"More than that, Mr. Brekov. My father and mother and I as a small child were taken to the concentration camp at Madigan. But my loyalty is not to people who drop atom bombs or make concentration camps or wipe out free speech and free press as you do. No, not at all. My loyalty is to the human species, which century after century suffers the malignant stupidity of men like yourself and your masters. I hate spies and I loathe your K.G.B. as much as I loathe our C.I.A. And my distaste for those organizations and what they stand for is so great that even if I knew where Robert Mackenzie is, I would not tell you."

"Hear! Hear!" a voice cried. "Bravo, Masuto! Turn around, Brekov, but slowly, carefully."

He had been hidden by Brekov's legs. Now, as Brekov stepped aside, Masuto saw him, Mackenzie at last, and recognized him though he had never seen him before. He held a heavy automatic pistol in his hand, and he said to Brekov, "Back up. Move in back of Masuto there." Mackenzie stood between the open French doors, just inside the meditation room. "If you're thinking of that idiot Thatcher, Brekov, and of him charging in here to rescue you, forget it. Mr. Thatcher is dead, very dead. Before Feona died, she confessed that Thatcher had done the job with her. So now I've evened it out, haven't I, you loathsome bastard. Can you believe that Thatcher was stupid enough to let me get into the car with him and to congratulate me on my readiness to give myself up. He saw you getting him the Order of Lenin. It was the last thing he saw before I strangled him. You know, I have only one regret—that I have to kill Masuto here. The poor yellow bastard did me no harm, but he's a witness—"

He was cut off by a voice that roared, "Police! Drop it, Mackenzie!"

Mackenzie spun around and flung a shot toward the French door to Ana's room. Beckman shot through the door, hitting Mackenzie in the chest, and as Mackenzie collapsed, the gun falling from his hand, Beckman was shouting, "Don't touch your gun, Brekov, or I'll kill you where you stand!"

Brekov smiled and raised both hands. Masuto untangled himself from the lotus position, picked up Mackenzie's gun, and then Beckman came through the French door.

"Sy, thank you," Masuto said to him.

"Believe me, I do not have a gun," Brekov said. "I never carry a gun."

Beckman was bent over Mackenzie. "He's dead."

Masuto ran his hands over Brekov. He had no gun.

"You saved my life," Brekov said to Beckman.

"I'm Jewish," Beckman snarled. "You hear me, you son of a bitch, I'm Jewish! So don't thank me!"

"You're also an accessory to two murders," Masuto said to Brekov. "Mackenzie's brother and a policeman named Clint."

Brekov shrugged. "I have diplomatic immunity. And since what I came here for has been accomplished, there is no reason for me to remain. So I say good night, Mr. Masuto."

"Is that right?" Beckman demanded indignantly.

"I'm afraid so," Masuto said. "But you'll have to wait here, Mr. Brekov, until the Culver City police get here. Apparently, there's a dead man in your car across the street, and you can't walk away from either him or the car."

"You have no right to hold me here."

"Goddamn you, shut your mouth and sit down!" Beckman yelled. "Your immunity won't keep me from beating the shit out of you. Just sit down and try not to be a total asshole." Beckman was shaking now. He took off his jacket and covered Mackenzie. "I won't sleep for a week. Why do we go on with this lousy job, Masuto?"

Masuto poured a glass of gin, neat. "Get this down."

Beckman gulped it, coughed, and said, "You call the cops and Wainwright, Masao. I can't talk to anyone."

"The Culver City cops, the captain, the State Department, the C.I.A., the F.B.I.—I know what you mean, Sy. Oh, the hell with it. I might as well start calling."

It was four o'clock in the morning before it was all finished, and the Culver City cops and the Beverly Hills cops and the two F.B.I. men and the man from the C.I.A. had all finished and departed, and Beckman had gone home to his wife, and the bodies had been removed, and Brekov had taken his diplomatic immunity back to Washington—and that was when Masuto finally got to cleaning up. He swept up the bits of glass and then scrubbed at the vinyl floor until the bloodstains were gone. There were two bullet holes in Ana's door and a bullet hole in the wall of her room—from the single wild shot Mackenzie had gotten off. Wainwright had given him the following day off, if he made up the time, which he promised to do. He decided that he would sleep for three hours, then find a glazier and have the glass replaced, cover the bullet hole with some plaster of Paris, and then drive out to Uncle Toda's place.

Perhaps if he got there early enough, he could bring Kati and the kids home before dark.